Look for the other books in the

Book of Nightmares

John Peel

AN
APPLE
PAPERBACK

SCHOLASTIC INC.
New York Toronto London Auckland Sydney

Cover art by Michael Evans

ISBN 0-590-14966-0

12 11 10 9 8 7 6 5 4 3 2   8 9/9 0 1 2 3/0

Printed in the U.S.A.   40
First Scholastic printing, April 1998

This is for Joe Pierro.
Thanks for all the help.

PROLOGUE

"Well," said Blink, trying to hide his yawn behind a large red paw, "that was something of a disaster, wasn't it? When's dinner?"

Shanara glared at her red panda angrily. "Is your stomach the only thing you can think of?" she demanded, her face almost as red as her hair. "Pixel's been kidnapped and taken to Zarathan, and food's the only thing on your mind?"

Shrugging, Blink settled down to rest. "Well, I think better on a full stomach," he grumbled. "But if there's not going to be any food, I'm going to catch up on my sleep. All *you'll* be doing is talking, and that doesn't interest me."

"Some days," Shanara growled to Oracle, "I am *very* tempted to turn him into stone. That way he'd *never* have to wake up again."

Oracle laughed. "But losing his help would reduce your powers, my dear," he reminded her. "You're a team."

"You have no idea how reluctant a team sometimes," she muttered. "I'm sorry to hear that Pixel's been kidnapped, but I suppose we should look on the good side — at least Score is restored to his full health again."

Oracle nodded. "Yes. He and Helaine are in fine shape, and both eager to rescue their captive friend."

"On the most dangerous world of the entire Diadem," Shanara reminded him. "This is one world from which even they may not be able to return."

Oracle shrugged. "Do you think that will deter them?"

"No," Shanara admitted. "They are all very loyal to one another. You have to admire that in them."

"I do," Oracle answered. "It's hard to believe that these three youngsters were once the Triad, isn't it? They're so unlike those destroyed despots — thank goodness! But it seems as if they can never escape all of the Triad's magic. Destiny used to work for them once, too, I gather. I never met her myself, but the Triad were full of secrets — from one another, as well

2

as from other people — so that's not surprising. But she's obviously clever, nasty, and powerful. And she's gone to Zarathan deliberately, even though she knows what it is."

"It's always possible," Shanara pointed out, "that she went on from there. She may not actually still be there."

"But we need to know," Oracle said. "That's why Helaine and Score are preparing to go there. If Pixel is still there, he's in deadly danger."

"Yes." Shanara was grim. "Zarathan is one world where even Blink wouldn't dare fall asleep. There, nightmares are real. And death lurks in every dream. Pixel is in serious trouble if he even yawns. And there's no way he could possibly know that. I'm sure Destiny hasn't told him."

"Then it's vital he's rescued quickly," Oracle agreed. "Otherwise, he'll sleep his way to death. . . ."

CHAPTER 1

Score was very agitated, and it was difficult for him to be still even for a moment. The events of the past couple of hours had been too much for him, one thing piled onto another. He'd been attacked magically, through a locket that had once belonged to his mother. It contained a photo of her and a lock of Score's baby hair from his first-ever trip to the barber. Using this, Destiny had managed to drain his strength and had almost killed him. Pixel and Helaine had risked their own lives to save Score, and they had succeeded in recovering the locket and breaking the death-spell.

But it had left Score terribly weak. As much as he'd objected to the delay in rushing off to help Pixel, Score had reluctantly realized that he was in no shape to help anyone. He'd been hungry and dehydrated, and stopping for a very large snack and a couple of gallons of soda and water had been essential. He'd wolfed down the food as if it were going out of style. Now he felt a whole lot better, at least physically.

The trip to Earth had left Score with more problems than ever. He'd run into his father again. That was never a happy event. His father, Bad Tony Caruso, was a crook, a bully, and a liar. But he'd also stunned Score by wanting to train him to take over his criminal organization. Score had naturally refused, but the offer had startled him.

Being on the verge of death, Score had not been afraid of his father — the first time in his life he could ever have said that. The fear had been burned out of him at last, and Score now realized that Bad Tony was actually a pretty pathetic excuse for a human being. Right now, he was back in police custody, where he would hopefully stay for a few years. Score liked the idea that he might be able to return to Earth sometime without running into his father. But at least now it was because he despised the man, not because he feared him.

Score had come to realize that there were questions about his mother to which he didn't know the answers. Bad Tony had mentioned that she was a *strega,* a wise woman from the old country. She had somehow known what Score was, and had prepared for his arrival. She'd died when Score was young, and he'd always assumed that Bad Tony had caused her death. Now, however, he wasn't so sure.

Bad Tony had been cruel with his son because he thought this would make a man out of Score. Bad Tony's own father had treated him the same way. But he swore he'd never been bad to Score's mother, and Score didn't think his father had been lying. Still, Score remembered his mother as being constantly afraid.

If not of Bad Tony, then of whom?

Score knew he'd have to go back to Earth to get answers to those questions. Who had his mother *really* been? And who had killed her?

Still, as disturbing as these questions were, they were not the most important things to focus on right now. The main problem at hand was Pixel. He was trapped by Destiny on the world of Zarathan, which apparently gave everyone the creeps. Well, it didn't make any difference. Pixel had risked his life to save Score and Score couldn't back out on his friend now, no matter what the odds.

Feeling much stronger once he'd eaten, Score left the room he'd been staying in. Right after the battle on Earth, Score and Helaine had returned to the world of Treen. They had taken over the wizard Aranak's tower — Aranak had no use for it now, since Helaine had been forced to kill him to save their lives. Most of Aranak's spells had expired with him, so the tower wasn't as magically convenient as it once had been. On his first visit to the tower, Score had been able to get food simply by calling out in the dining room for whatever he wished. Now, it all had to be brought in.

Luckily, the local Beastials had realized that Score and Helaine had returned. The Beastials were the half-humans who lived close to Aranak's tower. They had once served him, mostly out of fear, and had been the ones responsible for bringing Score, Helaine, and Pixel to Treen in the first place. They had sold out the three of them to save their own skins. As a result, they felt a mixture of shame and fear toward Score and Helaine. They'd brought food to the two travelers in a blatant attempt to get back on their good side. Still, the Beastials refused to enter the tower, even with Aranak's magic decayed, and were camped outside. Score didn't know whether this was because they were guarding the small party from the local humans — who loathed and feared any magic-users —

or simply because they wanted to look like they were being useful. To be honest, he didn't really care.

Score hurried back to the library, where Shanara was waiting for them. She'd been looking through Aranak's large collection of books while the trio had been on Earth, and had earmarked a few to take home with her when she left.

Helaine and Oracle were already there. Oracle was dressed completely in black, as always, and was flickering slightly. He wasn't exactly all there; he was a projection of a person, not a real, living being. But he had once served the Triad, the masters of the Diadem before they had fallen, and now he served Score, Helaine, and Pixel — on and off, and in his own rather odd fashion.

Helaine was as impatient to be off as Score was. She wasn't very good at keeping her temper, and Score could see that she was close to her boiling point right now. She was just as worried about Pixel as he was, if not more so. She'd taken the time to change, Score noticed. She hadn't much liked Earth clothing. She was from a medieval world where everyone covered up most of their bodies. She'd been shocked at the "indecent" clothing worn in New York. Even a T-shirt had been scandalous for her. She was back in her leather leggings, tunic, and the light chain mail she liked to wear over that. Her sword was once again strapped to her waist. She had hated having to leave that behind to go to Earth.

"Good," she said gruffly, glancing at him as he arrived. "You've finished eating. Are you ready to go?"

"Back in peak form," he assured her. "Ready for — well, as little trouble as possible." He sighed. "But I know better than to expect this to be a piece of cake."

She nodded, ignoring his comments, and turned back to Shanara. "Now we can go."

"Not quite yet," Shanara replied. "You may be physically ready for Zarathan, but mentally you're nowhere near ready. Zarathan is a world unlike any other in the Diadem. It's the most lethal world we know of. Nobody ever returns from there."

Score didn't like the sound of that, but he had no choice about going. He managed a weak smile. "Well, let's see if we can make that nobody *except* the four of us, then."

"Three," Helaine said darkly. "Shanara isn't coming with us."

Score frowned. Not coming with them? Well, she hadn't actually said that she would. But Score had assumed that this was the general idea. She hadn't been able to go with them to Earth because she'd had to stay on Treen to maintain the Portal between the two worlds. On Earth, Score, Helaine, and Pixel's powers had been too weak to open a Portal; it had to be opened from Treen. That was because Earth was one of the Outer Worlds, where magic was very weak. Treen was on the Outer Circuit, closer to the center of the Diadem, and their powers were stronger here. But Zarathan was also on the Outer Circuit, and opening a Portal there shouldn't be a problem at all. So Shanara didn't have to stay here and help them. "But I sort of thought . . ." Score said, his voice trailing off weakly. Was she too *scared* to come with them?

He didn't like to think that of her. Aside from the fact that she was a fellow magic-user and a friend, she was also drop-dead gorgeous. Score realized that this might not be her *actual* appearance, of course, because her specialty was creating illusions. The first time he'd seen her, she'd been dark-haired. When they'd set off for Earth, she'd been a blonde. Today she was a red-head. Changing her hair color was a snap for her, and she clearly enjoyed doing it. Maybe she'd changed her real appearance by magic, too. He didn't know, but he liked the way she looked. Having her along on an adventure would have made it . . . interesting.

"I'm sorry if my decision disappoints you," Shanara said gently. "But you *must* understand the dangers of Zarathan."

Helaine gave her a look of betrayal. "I did not think you were so afraid that you would not help us," she said in a hurt voice.

"It's not *fear* that keeps me from helping you," Shanara said, an edge of anger in her voice. "It's *sense.* Listen to me for a few minutes, and stop trying to get yourselves killed.

"Zarathan is a world where nightmares rule. It is a strange world, where nothing and everything is real at the same time. Somehow it can latch onto your thoughts and bring them to life. And they become terribly real. They can kill you. But that is not the worst part of Zarathan. If you start to doze, or, worst of all, sleep, then you are doomed. The planet can rip the soul out of your body through your dreaming. You will never awaken, and never be whole. You will be trapped forever as dreaming ghosts."

Score shuddered. "Okay, I'm scared clear through to the bone. Thanks a heap. So we can't sleep."

"It's not that simple," Shanara explained. "The world will be attacking you. Nobody knows why, or who is behind it, but the place drains your energies. That is why I insisted that you both eat good meals. You will need every ounce of strength to survive there. And it is why I cannot accompany you — I would weaken you too much."

Score scowled. Probably Pixel, with his agile

11

mind, would have known what Shanara was talking about, but he was totally lost. "I don't get it," he admitted. "Why would your presence hurt us?"

"Because my magic is mostly illusion," she explained. "The same kind of magic that rules on Zarathan. And my power comes in large part from Blink — who spends most of his time sleeping."

Helaine calmed down as this sank in. "Blink would be lost in seconds on Zarathan," she realized. "And you would not last much longer."

"No," Shanara agreed. "I'd be an anchor, dragging you back and weakening you. Whatever evil force it is that envelopes that world would feed off me and weaken you both. I dearly wish I could go with you to help save Pixel, but I can't."

"I understand," Helaine said. "And I'm sorry I was so nasty before."

"It's all right," Shanara answered.

Oracle made a face. "If anyone suggests a group hug," he said, "I'm going to throw up."

"That," Score commented, "would be interesting. If we tried to hug you, we'd pass right through you. And how would a projection barf, anyway?"

"I don't want to find out," Helaine said firmly. "Look, if that's all we need to know right now, then I think we'd better get a move on and create a Portal to Zarathan. Pixel doesn't know about the dangers of that world, and I doubt Destiny is going to clue him in. If she even knows about Zarathan."

"She knows," Oracle said grimly. "Even the Triad were scared of that world. No amount of magic can make you immune to its power, and they made certain that anyone who worked for them knew about its dangers."

Score frowned. "So, if Destiny knows what that place is like, what's she doing there?"

Shanara sighed. "My own guess is that she went there to decoy you. And that as soon as she arrived, she created another Portal to get off the planet again and head somewhere safer."

"So she may not even be there when we arrive?" asked Score. "Wow, this thing keeps getting better and better."

"A trap?" Helaine suggested. "It would make sense, and it is the sort of thing that she likes doing. Can't you tell if she's still there by using your scrying powers?"

Shanara shook her head. "My ability to see on Zarathan is almost zero. But once you get there, I can focus through your strength and try again. Then I should be able to tell you if they are still there, or if they've traveled onward."

"Well, that's something, at least," Score conceded. "*Now* can we go?"

"Outside," Shanara said. "Portals form easier in the open air."

That was some sort of magical rule, obviously. Score understood that such things made their own kind of sense. They *had* traveled through a Portal in their castle on Dondar, but on that planet their magic was a lot stronger, since it was on the Inner Circuit of worlds.

Outside, Shanara started the spell to make the gateway between worlds. Helaine and Score waited, having agreed to let her use her strength to make the Portal so that they could conserve their own strength for Zarathan.

Three of the assembled Beastials hovered close to them. These were the ones they had dealt with before — S'hee the killer whale man, Rahn the leopard woman, and Hakar the eagle man. They all looked vaguely human, but with tinges of their beast-natures.

"We wish you good hunting," Rahn said, her fangs glinting in the sun.

"And good fortune," rumbled S'hee, shifting his black-and-white body rather nervously.

"And a safe return," added Hakar, his voice slightly distorted because of his beak. He had once been trapped as a hawk, but was back as a Beastial now that the magic in the Diadem had been fixed.

14

"Thanks," said Score dryly. "You always seem to be here to see us off your world. Terrific."

"It is not our fault," S'hee said nervously.

"We know," Helaine agreed. "But it does not endear you to us. Perhaps one day we might be able to be friends. But this is not the day."

Score suddenly felt the crackle of magic in the air, and spun about to where Shanara had conjured up the Portal. The jagged-edged blackness crackled in the crisp air.

"Now," Shanara said. "Be bold, and be fortunate!"

"Be a round-trip ticket," Score begged the Portal as he threw himself through the blackness right behind Helaine.

They emerged into the strangest world he had ever seen.

CHAPTER 2

Tendrils of mist crawled about Helaine's feet as she stared intently all around her. Aside from Score, standing a few feet away, and a small circle of soil, she could see nothing. Mist and fog seethed around them. The air was damp and chilly, and she couldn't help shivering.

"New Jersey on the weekends," Score muttered. It was obviously some sort of a joke, but Helaine wasn't very amused.

"I don't like this place," she admitted, scanning all around and seeing nothing. "In this fog, anything could be waiting just out of sight. If we were attacked, we wouldn't know it until it was upon us."

"Boy, you're a ray of sunshine," Score complained. "Anyway, if we can't see anything, then anything out there can't see us, either, can it? We're all blind together. So what do we do?"

Helaine shrugged. "We may as well start walking. I'll contact Shanara, and see if she's detecting anything through our link." She placed her hand on her agate, the jewel that helped her to communicate with others telepathically. *Shanara?* she called out mentally. *Are you able to find anything out yet?*

Not a lot, came back the clear reply. *I don't think Destiny or Pixel has left Zarathan yet, but it's hard to see. I get the impression that if you travel east, you'll find them. But I don't know how far.*

Thanks, Helaine answered. *But we don't have any idea which direction is east on this world. There's fog all around us, and we can't see farther than about six feet.*

Not a problem, Shanara replied. *I'm not bound by the fog. East is off on your left now. I'll keep trying to see if I can find anything else out.*

Helaine broke contact and gestured for Score. "Shanara says we should head east. She's pretty sure they're still here, but can't be more specific."

Score sighed. "I might have known nothing would be easy." He fell in beside Helaine. "Why can't just

17

one of our problems have a simple solution for a change?"

"Where would the challenge be in that?" Helaine asked.

"Some of us don't need constant challenges to make us happy," Score answered. "I'd love the quiet life myself."

"You would get bored and out of shape," Helaine informed him. "Not that you're in great shape right now."

"Yeah, and I love you, too," he told her sarcastically.

Helaine felt uncomfortable. She'd not really meant to insult him, just to tell the truth. Score wasn't a warrior, as she was. He wasn't in shape, as she was. She knew that this wasn't necessarily a terribly bad thing, but sometimes he frustrated her in his overly casual attitude. On the other hand, he was remarkably effective with magic, and had changed a great deal since they had first met up. He was no longer the coward he had been, and was toughening up a bit. Helaine didn't know how she could possibly say all of this to him without him taking it the wrong way. She settled for a grunt instead — and found her face slightly red. For some reason, he was unsettling her, and she didn't know why.

As they walked, a terrible screeching sound suddenly came from the distance. It then cut off just as quickly as it had begun.

"The natives are getting restless tonight," Score muttered. "Was that human, animal, or monster?"

"I don't know," Helaine admitted. "Whatever it was, it sounded as if it was in terrible pain." She felt so helpless, being unable to see more than a few feet ahead of her. Another scream came, this one longer and more pain-filled than the first. Then a whole series of chattering sounds, almost like human laughter, filled the air. This was followed by another scream and then silence.

"Okay," Score decided, "I am *definitely* not taking my vacation here this year."

Helaine knew he was joking to cover up his nervousness. "We'd better move on," she suggested. "The sounds are coming from the south, so we shouldn't be getting too close to whatever caused them."

"Unless they're on the move, too," Score pointed out.

That was a thought she didn't need. Silently, she moved off again, and Score fell in close behind. There were further noises, but not as loud or as close. Still, it was clear that something was hunting on this world, and that made Helaine grip the pommel of her sword, ready to draw it at any second.

The ground rumbled slightly beneath their feet. It was just enough to make them shake unsteadily, but not enough to knock them down.

"Oh, great," Score complained. "We're in an earthquake zone on top of everything else."

"Look on the bright side," Helaine suggested. "At least we're outdoors. Nothing to fall on you if there's a big quake."

He pointed to the ground, and she saw a spider-web of tiny cracks in the baked earth. "There's nothing to stop us from falling to our deaths if that splits."

"Then we'd better move," she suggested. "The sooner we are off this planet, the happier we'll all be." With the ground still trembling slightly, she quickened her pace.

Helaine realized something. The ground was bare dirt and rock. They hadn't passed any trees, plants, or grass. Nothing seemed to live here — yet something had made those screams. How could there be any sort of animal life or human life if there were no plants? There was nothing for any creature to eat here.

This world made her skin crawl. And that really disturbed her. Helaine wasn't used to being frightened. She'd been scared plenty of times, but that wasn't the same thing. If you were confronted by a fire-breathing dragon, you'd have to be a total idiot not to feel scared. But *frightened* was another matter. It was apprehension that clutched at her, worry that something was stalking them and fear that, whatever it was, she wouldn't be able to deal with it.

And that was what bothered her. She was being spooked by noises and shadows, and she'd never felt that way before. Back home at Votrin Castle, the young girls were all supposed to be shy and timid creatures, in order to make the men feel brave and strong in defending them. Helaine had never believed in that for a second. She didn't need anyone to fight on her behalf; she could stand up for herself. So she'd never bought into being shy and nervous. On the contrary, she was forceful and self-sufficient. Except for now. What was wrong with her?

She cast a glance at Score and saw that he was just as bothered as she was. Well, that was no surprise. He'd been trying his best to be brave, but it was difficult for him to overcome a lifetime of fear. This place must be even scarier for him that it was for her. But *why* was she so scared? It wasn't like her. It was as if she was somehow in tune with Score's fears.

And then she realized what was happening.

"I think we're picking up some sort of low-level telepathic message," she informed Score. "Something or someone is broadcasting fear to us, making us nervous and afraid."

"I've got news for whoever or whatever's doing it," Score told her. "They're wasting their time — I can be quite scared without any help." Then he nodded. "But I think you're right; even I'm not normally *this* bad." He wiped his sweaty palms down his jeans' legs.

"Well, now that we know it's happening, we can fight back against it," Helaine said.

"*You* can," Score muttered. But he made an obvious effort to drag his courage back together.

They went on. It was impossible for them to be sure how far they had traveled, or how long they'd been walking. The mists never cleared. And the light around them stayed constant. It was still daytime, and there was no sign of night approaching. That was a good thing; the idea of spending a night awake on this world didn't appeal to Helaine at all. The screams, harsh laughter, and howls came and went from time to time. The ground shook beneath their feet at intervals.

"This is weird," Score pointed out after another of the small shocks. "I've been counting. The last two quakes were exactly four and a half minutes apart. And so were the two previous ones."

Helaine frowned as she realized what he was saying. "The quakes are timed regularly?"

"Every four and a half minutes," he answered. "Either this planet is run by clockwork, or there's something seriously bizarre going on." He gave her a nervous smile. "So, let's see if the next quake happens exactly on time."

They waited, standing still and alert. After precisely four and a half minutes, the ground shook again, a trembling beneath their feet.

"You're right," she told him. "This *is* weird. But I don't know what it means."

"It means we'd better get off this planet fast," he told her. "It means that I'm getting more scared by the minute."

"Come on." Helaine started off again, into the gloom. A few minutes later, she stopped. The quake came again, as expected. This disturbed her because she didn't know what it meant. Only that it had to be trouble, somehow.

Seeing something out of the corner of her eye, Helaine stopped so suddenly that Score bumped into her.

"Ouch," he complained. "I got the handle of your sword right in my stomach. What did you do that for?"

Helaine didn't need to answer. She simply pointed.

Finally, there was something new to see, instead of just dirt. There were two stones piled on top of each another. They had been cut into blocks, though the top one had broken apart. Moss was growing on them, showing they had been there for a long time.

"Life," Score said. "Well, at one time, anyway. A while ago, by the look of things."

Helaine nodded, and moved forward, past the two stones. Was it her imagination, or was the fog lifting slightly? She was sure she could see a little farther now — ten feet or so instead of six. There were more blocks, and then she knew she was right, because she could see a portion of a wall about fifteen feet ahead of them.

It was made from more of the chunks of stone. These were all encrusted with moss and stained from seepages. Still, it had to be a defensive wall of some kind. There was a small window about twenty feet up the wall, clearly intended as a place from which to fire arrows at an attacker.

Strangest of all, Helaine had an odd feeling she'd seen something like this before.

Score surveyed the wall with his usual mixture of worry and humor. "I guess nobody's home," he said. "Either that, or they really need to hire a new house-keeper." He looked at her. "You think this is where Destiny's got Pixel captive?"

Helaine shrugged. "We have to check it out," she answered. "But it's going to be in poor shape, so we'd better be very careful. If one of the stones or steps breaks beneath our feet, we could fall to our deaths."

"Has anyone ever told you that you have a sunny disposition?" Score asked her.

Helaine ignored his joke and moved forward again. There was no doubt that the fog wasn't as thick around the ancient stones. She could see a good deal of the castle walls now and had an idea where the main entrance must lie. "This way," she said, heading off to the left.

Directly ahead of them, outside the castle wall, was a small cemetery. It was obviously where the lord of the castle had buried his relatives. It was mostly in ruins now, with the stone markers cracked and unreadable. There were two large crypts, where the most important people had to be buried. Some long-forgotten lords and ladies of this blighted land. The crypts were still standing, but they were twisted out of shape, their stones discolored by age and neglect. Again, Helaine had the strangest feeling that she should recognize this place, even though she couldn't possibly have been here before.

There was a strange sound, a kind of a clattering noise. Helaine frowned, looking around to see where it might have come from. There was nothing in sight that might have produced any kind of noise. The only living or moving things around were her and Score.

But she could feel that there was trouble coming. That was a gift she possessed, the ability to know when she was going to be attacked. The problem was that it wasn't very specific — just a feeling of imminent danger. She drew her sword instinctively.

"I *hate* it when you do that," Score complained. "There's trouble on the way, right?"

"Right," she agreed, her eyes scanning all around. "Can't you hear that noise?" The clacking sound was growing louder.

"I had hoped it was just my teeth chattering," Score said slowly. "Is it just my imagination, or is it coming from the graveyard?"

"I wish it was just your imagination," Helaine replied. "But you're correct."

The sounds *were* coming from the small burial ground. She couldn't see anything at first, and then the door to one of the crypts gave a squeal as it was wrenched aside. Helaine gasped as she saw what was coming from the grave.

It was barely more than an animated skeleton. A few shreds of clothing hung from it, and a little hair was somehow still attached to the skull. It carried a steel sword in its right hand. Its bones were yellowed with age and cracked in several places. There was absolutely no way it should have been able to move at all. It had no muscles, or anything on the bones. Even on worlds where magic reigned, animating a skeleton was next to impossible.

The skeleton forced its way through the door, clacking its way as it walked toward them. Three more, all carrying swords, followed.

Helaine was almost too scared to move. This was beyond magic or science. It was *impossible.* Skeletons couldn't walk and carry swords. They were just broken bones!

Unfortunately, their attackers didn't seem to be aware of how impossible they were; they sprang forward, their swords waving, to the attack.

This broke the hold of fear that had gripped Helaine. Impossible foes or not, they were attacking her, and that was something she knew how to deal with. She blocked the blow of the first skeleton, then disengaged, whirling about to parry the thrust of the second. The other two closed in as well. Helaine looked for a way to strike back — and wondered how she could hurt something that was already dead. There was no vital spot to thrust for, no arteries to slash or muscles to cut. Only cold, dead bones . . .

Helaine was fighting for her life as three of them went for her at once. Somehow, she managed to dodge their blows and block their thrusts. All the time her mind kept insisting that this couldn't possibly be happening. The skeletons didn't even have eyes —

how could they see her to attack? She had no idea, but somehow they were managing it.

The final skeleton went for Score. Helaine couldn't spare more than a quick glance to make sure he was all right. He wasn't any good at hand-to-hand combat, but his fear seemed to have calmed to manageable proportions, and he was fighting with magic, hurling fire at his attacker. Helaine couldn't see that it would do much good against a dead foe, but she was too busy fighting off her own attackers to spare more than a thought for Score.

Being dead, her opponents didn't seem to get tired — unlike her. She was panting already, swinging, blocking, and parrying three swords. Her arms were aching from the blows that her sword was absorbing. She couldn't fight very long like this. She needed some way to kill the skeletons.

She thrust her sword through the rib cage of one skeleton, and did absolutely no damage whatsoever. As the one on her left tried to jump in, she whirled around and hacked out, both hands on the sword for extra strength.

Her blade cut through the skeleton's left arm. The arm clattered to the ground, twitching, trying to get back into the fight. But it couldn't. The skeleton looked down at the missing limb, and then attacked with its remaining arm.

That figured; it could hardly bleed to death from such a blow, or even, apparently, feel any pain. Still, it gave her an idea. Perhaps the skeletons couldn't be killed, but they *could* be broken apart. . . .

She singled out the one on her right, diving below its sword thrust and knocking its arm up. Then she swung her sword and hacked through its right leg. The leg flew aside, shattering into several pieces. The unbalanced skeleton collapsed. Helaine whirled to take on the remaining two, watching the fallen one out of the corner of her eye. It struggled to rise and rejoin the fight, but on only one leg it was having a great deal of trouble.

Then there was a huge burst of flame behind her, and Score whooped, "Got one! All riiiight!" Helaine saw that the skeleton that had been attacking him had been hit by an intensely hot fireball, which had charred most of it to dust.

"Cremation!" Score yelled. "The heat pulverizes the bones."

A clever thought. Helaine blocked another blow, her arms jarring from the force. Then she took off the skeleton's right arm, sending its sword flying. With both arms gone, the foe was powerless. She turned to take on the last standing skeleton, and that was a near-fatal mistake.

Unlike a human, the armless skeleton felt neither pain nor loss simply because its arms were gone. It ran and threw itself at her, feet first, and slammed into her back while she wasn't watching.

The heavy, unexpected blow sent Helaine crashing to the ground. She was momentarily stunned as the skeleton continued to dance painfully on her back. Then the last skeleton closed in, raising its sword to strike down at her.

An intense fireball slammed into the attacker, burning most of it to dust. Blackened shards of bone clattered to the ground, and Helaine heard Score whooping yet again.

Annoyed, she rolled over, sending the armless skeleton flying. She was on her feet instantly, if somewhat painfully. Snarling, she brought her sword down again and again on the injured skeleton, hacking it into tiny, twitching pieces. Then she did the same thing to the one she'd cut the leg from. Panting, she stood staring at the remains, which were shaking nervously, as if each part wanted to continue the attack but simply couldn't. She brushed the hair from her eyes and looked at Score. "Thank you."

"Anytime," he replied, a slightly mocking grin on his face. "I thought that one on your back was doing a really good macarena, though."

Helaine had no idea what he was talking about, and suspected that she didn't really want to know. She looked around for further danger, but everything was peaceful once again. She felt a great weariness, and the urge to just stop and rest for a bit.

She fought back the thought. "Our foe is at it again," she warned Score, seeing him yawning. "It's making us feel sleepy, and draining our energy."

"Oh, wonderful," Score said with a sigh. "It's trying to make us rest. And if we do, we die." He stared at the squirming bones. "And if we don't rest, I suspect there's more trouble ahead."

"We must go on," Helaine informed him. "We must find Pixel. Don't forget, he doesn't know about this planet. If he decides to take a break, he's doomed."

"Let's just hope he can hold out until we get to him," Score answered.

CHAPTER 3

Pixel tested the strength of the chains that joined him to the wall, and raised an eyebrow. "I guess you don't want me going anywhere," he said.

Destiny gave a short, sharp laugh. "Trust me, you wouldn't want to be away from me on this planet. It's a very dangerous place. You're much safer in here with me."

"Chained in the heart of a maze," Pixel added dryly. He rattled the chains again. "You can't imagine how safe this makes me feel."

Destiny laughed again. "I like you, Pixel. I really do. It's such a shame that I have to kill you, but . . ." She shrugged. "On Earth, they have a saying: You can't make an omelette without breaking a few eggs."

"And I'm the chosen egg?" Pixel was trying to keep his voice light, but he was badly worried. Destiny had brought him through to this strange planet with a knife at his throat. He'd attempted to free himself magically from her grasp, but had found it impossible for some reason. Whenever she got close to him, he could feel his powers ebbing. She had somehow brought him here, to this labyrinth, and he couldn't quite recall how she'd done it. On Earth, Destiny had not had much magical strength; crossing to Zarathan had definitely made her more powerful.

Right now, she was walking around the room with a delighted expression on her face. She saw him watching and laughed again. "You can't possibly imagine how good this feels," she told him. "I've been confined to a wheelchair all of my current life. To be able to walk again — it's astonishing."

"Then be generous," he suggested, without much hope. "Since we restored your freedom, restore mine."

"Nice try," Destiny commented. "But, sorry. I may be free, but I don't have what was taken from me by the Triad."

She had admitted that she had once worked for the Triad, and had been banished to Earth, labeled a traitor by the Three Who Ruled. They had drained her powers as punishment. She's been stuck on Earth for thirteen years in the form of a young wheelchair-bound Japanese girl. All that time, she'd been brooding and planning her escape. She had found out about Score and the locket, using it to draw him to her. When her plans had gone wrong, she'd been forced to take Pixel along as a hostage — and, it now appeared, much more.

"What do you plan on doing?" he asked her.

"Oh, no," Destiny answered. "If I tell you, then you're bound to try and work out some way to stop me. It's not possible to stop me, of course. But you and your friends are very resourceful, and you might at least hinder me. I've been waiting a long time for this, and I'm going to relish every moment of it." She smiled at him. "Stop messing around with those chains. You won't get free, and you'll just tire yourself out. Sit back and relax. Take a nap, if you like."

"Thanks," Pixel said. "But I don't think I could sleep in the same room as you. The stench would prevent me."

That wiped the smile off her face for a moment. "Suit yourself," she snapped. "But you'll be here for a while. It really would make more sense for you to rest and conserve your strength."

"For what?" he asked her.

She shook her head. "Sorry, can't tell you." Then she smiled again. "But it has something to do with this planet. Many people hate and fear it, but I've always felt a certain attraction to it. It has so much raw power. Now, I'll have to leave you alone for a little while. I have a certain . . . *ritual* to prepare for, and it will need a great deal of concentration on my part. Much as I like you, Pixel, you can be quite distracting with your constant questions. Try to behave while I'm gone, and I promise you a starring role in the upcoming ritual."

"Somehow," he muttered, "I doubt I'll like it."

"No," she agreed. "You probably won't. *Ciao.*" She blew him a mocking kiss and then left the central room.

Pixel looked around. He knew that he was in a labyrinth only because she had told him so. All he had seen was the room he was now in. It was about ten feet across, and eight tall, constructed of old, worn stones. There was the sound of dripping water constantly in the background. The only light in the place was from three torches set in sconces in the wall, all burning fitfully and casting long, intense shadows.

There was only one exit, the gap in the wall through which Destiny had left. The only thing in the room with him was a small, rickety table over by the exit. On this, Pixel could see his gemstones. Destiny had carefully taken them from him and placed them tantalizingly close, although still out of range of his powers. He couldn't use them to get himself free. However, if he could get free, then they'd be close at hand for him to grab.

The first question, then, was: Could he get free?

He examined the two chains that held him to the wall. They were threaded through a ring set into the stone, and each chain ended with a band about his wrist. These bands had been locked with a key that Destiny had slipped into her pocket.

And that was very odd. Pixel couldn't help himself; it was in his nature to puzzle things out, and this was certainly a puzzle. Destiny had been trapped on Earth for thirteen years. Yet when she had arrived here, she had somehow known about this maze, and she had a key to the locks that bound him. How was that possible? He couldn't see any logical answer right now, so he ignored the question and started to work on a plan of escape.

The crystals were so tempting that he tried time and again to reach them. But it was no use. He could feel his power fizzle before it reached the table. It was as if there were some sort of dampening field on the whole place, sucking the magic away. So using the crystals to get free was out. Next possibility?

He examined the bands around his wrists. They were tight and a lot more modern than the labyrinth. They were clean and polished. He examined the chain link by link, looking for a weak one that he might somehow be able to break. But they all looked as if they'd only been made that very day — bright, clean, and strong. There was no way to break the chain.

Picking the lock? Pixel didn't know how to do such a thing. Score probably would, but he wasn't available. Pixel's knowledge of the real world was rather limited. He'd spent most of his time on his home world of Calomir in Virtual Reality. That was fine for learning stuff and playing around, but it had very little connection to surviving in the real world.

Especially surviving murder attempts by insane magic-users.

When he'd first met Destiny, he'd been charmed by her. What an idiot he'd been! She'd completely fooled the three of them, and now she had some weird plan to get extra power from him. Aranak had tried something like this, and it had involved draining and then murdering the three of them. Pixel suspected Destiny's plans would have similar goals. He had no idea how long she'd be out of the room, but he couldn't rely on it being very long.

He knew it was time to think. He couldn't use the crystals, he couldn't break the chains, and he couldn't pick the lock. Well, that didn't leave too many options, did it? What *could* he do?

He still had some of his magic power. He could do small stuff, even in this dampening field. A little levitation, maybe, but not enough to reach across the room and pick up a crystal. Making fire, certainly. But that wouldn't help at all. If he tried to use fire to melt his chains, he'd be in trouble. They were made of iron, and he'd burn himself to death before he melted them. So that was no good.

But wait — Pixel felt a sudden rush of hope as he realized that he *did* have something he could do with his fire-making ability. He didn't have to use it on his chains. . . . He calmed himself down and focused his energies on making fire. *Shriker Kula prior* — those were the words of the spell. Even though his power was lower than normal, he could feel the buildup of heat. Concentrating the fire into a ball, he formed it in the air in front of him and threw it.

The ball of fire hit the table leg and exploded into flames just as he had planned. The fireball was small but hot, and the table was old and dry. The leg burst into flames, and he grinned. *Yes!* It was working.

In minutes, the leg had burned through, and the tabletop caught fire. Pixel felt a momentary pang of worry, but realized that the flames wouldn't hurt his gems. Any second now . . .

The leg snapped, weakened by the fire, and the table pitched forward drunkenly.

The four gems toppled to the floor and rolled. Pixel held his breath, watching them sparkle and spin in the firelight. *Closer!* he willed them. Three of them spun to a halt outside his range, but the blue-green beryl came into useful distance. He could feel its strength flooding into him.

The beryl gave him the power to control the element of Air. So all he had to do was to figure out some way to use Air to free himself. Making a whirlwind wouldn't help, for example. It might tear his chains free, but it would more likely smash him senseless against the walls. No, he had to be cunning. . . .

And then he knew what to do. Iron *rusted.* This happened because oxygen in the air reacted with iron to make rust. Since he had control over Air, Pixel could speed up the whole process. Concentrating on the bands around his wrists, he intensified the action of rusting.

As he watched, a thin red sheen covered the surface of the polished metal, eating into it and flaking free. Sweat poured down his brow as he continued to concentrate. The bands rusted away until he was finally able to snap them open.

Pixel rubbed his wrists, relieved to be free. Quickly, he scooped up his four jewels and slipped them back into his pocket. Now his next task was to find a way out of the maze. He hurried to the gap in the wall and peered around the edge. There was no sign of Destiny, thank goodness. Instead he saw a short corridor, with a turn to the right. Gripping one of the torches, Pixel set off and peered around the corner.

It was a T-junction; which way should he go?

He pulled out his ruby and focused. This gave him the power to find whatever he wanted. "S'erehw eht rood tuo fo ereh?" he asked the power. (Using the ruby made him communicate backward on some worlds.) Instantly, a red beam shot to the left. He could follow the beam mentally, and saw that there was an old oak door at the end of the maze that would lead him to freedom.

All he had to do was to get there. With his ruby, that shouldn't really be a problem. All he had to was use it to find the correct path to take. This escape was going to be dead easy. And once he was out of the labyrinth, he could see about contacting Score and Helaine. He knew they wouldn't leave him here alone. They were bound to come after him. Once they were together again, everything would be fine.

Grinning happily, he hurried down the left-hand passageway. Once Destiny was focused and ready for her ritual, she'd head back to the heart of the maze, only to find him gone. She'd seriously underestimated him, and she'd be really mad. . . .

Which made him feel good.

Destiny watched as Pixel hurried down the corridor away from where she was hiding. She couldn't help grinning. The little idiot had taken longer to free himself than she'd expected, but so what? He was free, thinking he was brave and smart and resourceful.

He didn't realize that this was exactly what she'd wanted him to do. As if leaving his crystals in the same room with him was an accident or an oversight! She knew he'd figure out some way to use them to free himself. And now he was off on a search for the way out of the labyrinth. Well, he'd never find it.

All she needed to do was to follow close behind him. Using his magic this wastefully was going to tire him out pretty quickly. He was bound to need to stop for a rest soon. And when he did, she'd have exactly what she needed. . . .

CHAPTER 4

Score walked very carefully away from the graveyard, shuddering. There was something really unsettling about fighting animated skeletons. It reminded him too much of all the fantasy films he'd seen on TV as a kid. He'd always thought that skeletons coming to life was silly, not scary. He'd just changed his mind.

Helaine was wordless, her face tight with tension. But she wasn't letting any of it out. She simply led the way around the castle wall. Above them was a tower, but it looked decidedly unsafe. Given a good wind, it might blow over. Portions of its walls were missing, and it was stained and smelled pretty rancid. Score stayed as far from it as possible.

They approached what he realized was the front of the castle. The walls here seemed to be in a bit better repair, and there was a massive gateway. At one time, there had been a moat around the castle, but it had drained away a long time ago, leaving only baked earth in the ditch. There weren't even any weeds. It seemed like the only things living here — aside from him and Helaine — were the dead. At one time, there had been a drawbridge connecting the castle to the roadway before it. But it must have rotted away a long time ago.

As they walked toward the gate, Score suddenly realized that Helaine was really bothered by something. This was so unusual that at first he thought he must be making a mistake. Then he peered again and discovered that she looked like she'd seen a ghost. Well, in this place, maybe she had.

"What's wrong?" Score asked. "Trouble?"

"Yes," Helaine replied, her voice almost breaking. She sounded as if she were on the verge of tears, which didn't make any sense at all. It was just so completely unlike Helaine. Score couldn't imagine anything that would make her cry. "But it's not the sort of trouble you're thinking," she added. They had reached the front gate now, and she gestured up. "I know this place."

He gazed at the gateway, which was large and deep. There were rusted chains hanging at the root of where the drawbridge must have once stood. A portcullis had crashed down, perhaps centuries earlier, and rotted through in several places. Over the gateway, some sort of coat of arms had been carved.

"You *know* this place?" Score asked, amazed.

"Yes." Helaine's eyes sparkled with unshed tears. "I should; it's my home."

"Your home?" Score stared at the ruins again. "No offense, Your Ladyship, but this is really a first-class *dump.* And you live here?"

"Idiot," she replied. "Not like *this,* I don't. My home is a living, vibrant place. But, somehow . . ." She gestured at the ruins. "That's our family coat of arms, and this is my father's castle. Or, rather, it looks like it *was,* a long time ago."

"Okay, time out," Score said, feeling very confused. "We're on Zarathan, not Ordin. Now, maybe we've somehow been catapulted to your home planet and into the far future, but I doubt it." He gestured all around him. "You're way too much of a snob to be caught dead in a dump like this."

That managed to cheer her up slightly, as he'd hoped it would. He didn't think he'd want to cope with a depressed Helaine. "Look," he went on, "I know this place *looks* like your home, but I don't think it really is. I think it's some kind of illusion, conjured up just to depress you. Don't let it work."

Helaine thought about what he'd said, and then walked toward the moat gap. On this side were two small pillars, obviously once part of the decor. She slapped the closest. "This is very real for an illusion," she pointed out.

"Maybe it is," he said. "Maybe you just think it is. Look, we don't know how strong Destiny's powers are likely to be on this planet, but doesn't it make more sense that this is something she's conjured up, rather than that we're somehow back at your little cottage in the woods?"

Helaine managed a weak smile. "Yes," she agreed. "Though I can't imagine how she'd know what my home looks like."

"Hey, she's a magician," Score pointed out. "Maybe reading minds is her special trick."

"Well," Helaine said firmly, "I'm going to act as though this *isn't* really Votrin Castle, and hope we're right. Still, there's one good thing about this."

"And what's that?" asked Score.

"At least she picked my home to wreck, and not yours. I don't think I could stand another trip to New York City so soon after the first."

Score grinned. "Aw, if she *had* picked New York, we'd have never known if it was decayed or not. Certainly not where I used to live, anyway." He was glad to see Helaine had cheered up again. "So, do we go in and scope the place out? Do we get to see your bedroom? It's not all done out in pink and cream, with pictures of rock stars on the walls, is it?"

Helaine looked disgusted. "Pink and cream?" she echoed. "Ugh. And what are *rock stars*? Don't they have normal stars in the sky in New York? How would a rock star shine?"

"I've often wondered that myself," Score muttered. He followed her down the slope of the moat. "Rock stars aren't really rocks or stars. They're musicians."

Helaine frowned. "Like minstrels? Then why do you call them what they're not?" She'd reached the bottom and started across to the far slope.

"I'll explain some other time," he told her. "Next time we go to Earth, I'm going to have to play you some tapes. You never know, you might like some of the stuff."

She gave him a funny look. "Are you trying to romance me? To — how do you say it on your world? — ask me out?"

"No!" Score exclaimed quickly. "Believe me, this is as far out with you as I want to go! I mean . . . well, you know what I mean." How could she possibly imagine he meant anything like *that*?

"I think I do," she agreed.

Was it his imagination, or did she look a little disappointed? He shook his head. He had to be imagining it; Pixel was the one who was soft on her. He concentrated on climbing up the far side of the moat. Helaine clambered up a lot faster than he did, then stood waiting for him at the top. Together, they managed to slip through one of the gaps in the portcullis and enter the courtyard.

The inside of the castle was just as run-down as the outside. Several of the walls had collapsed, leaving gaping holes in the masonry. "Well, this should save some time," Score commented. "We can see right through some of these rooms. So, where do we start?"

"The dungeon," Helaine suggested. "It's the logical place to put a prisoner, and it's down below, so it's less exposed to the elements."

"A *dungeon*?" Score asked, appalled. "Your father kept people in a *dungeon*?" He shook his head. "Some family you come from."

Helaine whirled angrily toward him. "Don't you *dare* speak against my family," she told him coldly. "The Votrins are one of the most noble families on Ordin."

"Noble, maybe," Score said, refusing to back down. "But barbaric. Keeping people in a dungeon . . ."

47

"Where else would you keep criminals and captives?" Helaine asked. "If someone has fought against you or betrayed your trust, you'd hardly show them to the guest quarters."

"It depends which world you're on," Score answered. "Anyway, how come you're defending the guy who was trying to marry you off to a half-wit?"

"My father and I had our . . . disagreements," Helaine said with dignity. "But I still love him. And my family's honor is very important. I won't let you speak ill of it. And, besides, he was more like a quarter-wit."

Score grunted. "There's just one teeny little thing you're forgetting," he pointed out. "You may have been born into the Votrin family, but you're not *really* a Votrin. The Triad just used your mother as a convenient host. So, whatever else you are, you can be sure you're not really descended from that great, noble stock."

For a second, Score honestly thought she was going to punch his lights out. Helaine was furious, and she pulled back her fist. Then she let it drop. Her shoulders drooped, and she bowed her head.

"You're right," she said quietly. "I'm a fool. I knew it, but I hadn't thought it through. I'm *not* really a Votrin, am I? I'm *Eremin*, whoever she was. I'm not really of noble birth. For all I know, I could be gutter-scum, like —" She broke off abruptly.

"Like me?" he asked, gently. "It's okay, you can't insult me." He sighed. "You know, it's funny. When I realized that I wasn't really Bad Tony's son, the knowledge set me free. I wasn't garbage, a crook by birth. Okay, I don't know who I *really* am, but I'm really glad I'm not Bad Tony's real son. You, on the other hand, were so proud of what you were. Daughter of a lord of Ordin and all that jazz. Now . . ."

"Now, I'm *nothing*," she said firmly. She looked up, and he saw that there actually were tears in her eyes. "I'm such a fool! I should have realized this long ago. I'm *nothing*!"

Score grabbed her firmly by the shoulders. "Get a grip," he ordered. "Let me tell you something, Helaine. It doesn't matter who your parents were, you're *you*. And you're definitely the most brave and noble person I've ever known. So your genes aren't from the high and mighty Votrin family. Big deal. It's what you are inside that makes you a person, and you've got what it takes." Then he grinned. "Of course, you've also got a lot of stuff inside you that makes you a royal pain."

That made her smile a little. "You really think so?" she asked, her voice a little stronger.

"That you're a pain? Trust me on that one."

"Not that — the other stuff," she said, frowning. "The brave and noble part."

49

"Yes," he said sincerely. "I meant it. You really are the most brave and noble person I know."

"Thank you," she said, and stood a little taller.

"I meant the other bit, too," he added. "So don't go thinking you're perfect." Score grinned. "But there's nobody I'd trust with my life more than you. And Pixel. Speaking of Pixel, we're supposed to be looking for him, remember? Not standing around discussing your family background."

"Right." Helaine had pulled herself together again. "But one of these days I want to find out who Eremin was. Maybe I *do* have family out there somewhere. And I still feel as though the Votrins are my family."

"So you were adopted," Score told her. "In a rather unique fashion. Big deal. Now, where are these dungeons?"

She led him to one of the sidewalls. There was a flight of steps leading down into a pit. "There should be a grating here," she explained. "But I guess it rotted away. Anyway, watch your footing. These steps are probably slimy."

She was right. Score followed her down very carefully. The steps led to a short passage, and then three doorways opened off it. The doors, like all the wood in the place, had rotted through a long time ago. The cells were small, with only a tiny hole in the center of the floor and small slits in the tops of the walls to let a little light through. It was obvious that nobody had been here for a long, long time.

"Not even rats," Score commented. "So, where next?"

"The ground-floor rooms, I guess," Helaine answered. She led the way back up. Score was glad to be out in the open again. It was hardly fresh air, but it was better than the dank odor of the cells. "This way to the main hall," she said, crossing the courtyard.

She didn't need to go inside this part of the castle. Judging from what was left, it had been a two-story portion, but the roof had fallen in and the whole thing was simply rubble.

"Wooden floors," Helaine explained. "Like everything else, they just rotted away."

"Makes searching simpler," Score said. He followed her as she entered a small doorway close to the main hall. This led into a doorway-filled passageway that was still pretty intact. "Shall we split up to check the place?"

"Stay with me," Helaine said. "I don't like the idea of splitting up here. If Destiny or whoever can create an illusion of my father's castle, who's to say they can't create doubles of us, too?"

"There's a horrible thought," Score commented. "Two of you."

"Two of *you*," she responded.

"You're right," he agreed. "That's *much* worse than two of you. Okay, we stay together."

The rooms were musty, disgusting, and stained by dripping water. Together, Score and Helaine checked out whatever remained intact of the ground floor. There were no signs of life at all. Then Helaine reached a stairway up that was relatively intact.

"Be very careful," she told him. "Test every step." She herself moved slowly up the spiral stone case. It was slippery, but he managed to keep his footing. He was glad when they stood on the second floor, though. With Helaine leading the way, they checked the rooms as they came to them. Many walls on this floor had collapsed, either into the courtyard or out over the moat. Gaps were everywhere, and the wind howled through them. It was like exploring a haunted castle.

Helaine stopped in the doorway of one room. Part of the far wall had collapsed, but it was slightly more intact than most. "My room," she said simply.

"Needs a touch of redecorating," he said. "Even if it's not pink and cream."

She smiled, and pointed to the left wall. "My bed was there. A four-poster. My trunk at its feet." She sighed. "I can't help missing my real room."

"I know," Score said. "But enough nostalgia — we still have to find Pixel."

They finished the floor off at the main tower. Helaine stood in the doorway and looked upward. "The floors have rotted through and collapsed," she reported. "There's nothing more in this section. Time to head down — the careful way."

They descended the spiral staircase again. "What's left?" he asked her.

"Quite a bit," she informed him. "This is a big, working castle. There are the stables, the black-smith's shop, the kitchens . . ."

"Speaking of which, I'm getting hungry again," Score muttered.

"I wouldn't eat anything on this world, if I were you," she told him seriously. "It might just try and eat you back."

"Charming thought." He followed her out into the courtyard, and then stopped suddenly. "Wasn't it af-ternoon when we went inside?"

Helaine glanced around and saw what he meant. Night was falling very suddenly. Shadows loomed large all around. "I guess we'll need light," she said. "But there's nothing to make a torch from."

"Hey, we're magicians," Score said. "How hard can it be to conjure up a ball of light?" He snapped his fingers and murmured the spell. A globe of fire appeared, bobbing up and down in the air, at about shoulder height. "It'll follow us like a faithful dog," he promised.

"Good. Let's . . ." She broke off suddenly. "Trouble." Then her sword was in her hand.

Score looked around but couldn't see anything. That sixth sense of hers for danger was a great help, but it was unspecific. What was happening?

He saw the answer a moment later, and remembered what he'd been thinking — that this was like a haunted castle.

Six transparent shapes moved toward them from the far side of the courtyard. They were a pale white, slightly luminescent. They were vaguely the shape and size of humans, but too indistinct to have any kind of features. Score shivered; he'd always hated ghost stories, and he had absolutely no doubt that he was now seeing a posse of ghosts.

Helaine looked almost as disturbed as he did. "Ghosts," she whispered, and there was more than a touch of fear in her voice.

"Nothing living here but the dead, remember?" he reminded her. His voice was a lot shakier than he liked. "They can't possibly hurt us, though — right?"

Helaine shook her head. "I'd like to believe that," she replied. "But if skeletons can come to life . . ."

"Don't say it," he begged her.

The six ghosts had drawn closer now. He could make out some details, even though they weren't quite all there. He could see some kind of elongated mouth and pointed teeth. Their eyes were a pale yellow, and slitted, like cats'. Their noses were like snouts. Their hands were more like claws.

"I've never heard of ghosts that looked like that before," he whispered to Helaine.

"I have," she answered, just as quietly. "They're called *tassim*. They drink the blood of their victims."

"Oh, great," Score muttered. "Dracula meets the spooks. Do you happen to know how you get rid of them?"

"You don't," Helaine replied. "You avoid meeting them."

"I think it's a little late for that," Score yelped as the *tassim* pounced. He punched out at the one closest to him. His fist went through it without effect. Then he felt tiny teeth jabbing into the skin of his arm and biting down. He yelled, and managed to shake the ghost free somehow. It scuttled away, licking its lips and teeth, now bright with specks of his blood. His arm hurt, and he could see blood trickling down it.

So could the other ghosts. With thin, reedy howls, they hurled themselves at Score and Helaine, greedy for blood. Helaine cried wordlessly, partly out of fear, and whirled her sword through them.

It had absolutely no effect on them.

Then the five ghosts cackled and attacked. Score felt two sets of teeth sinking into his skin, seeking his blood.

They couldn't touch the ghosts, but the ghosts could do more than touch — they could kill. . . .

CHAPTER 5

Helaine screamed in pain as one of the *tassim* chomped down on her thigh. With a snarl of rage, she shook it free. It scurried back a short distance, and then turned to come at her again. Another one came faster, fastening its teeth on her wrist. It was a painful bite, but she shook the ghost free.

"Think about these things!" Score yelled, shaking teeth free from his arm. "You must know something about them that might help us!"

"Not much," she replied. Another dived at her, biting her ankle right through her boot. She kicked out, and the ghoul flew off. "Just that they come out at night and drink your blood. It's an old children's story on my world."

"Why couldn't you have stories about ghosts that — ouch! — tickle people instead?" Score complained. "Why do they have to drink blood?"

"Because they want to become more real," Helaine answered as one bit her hand. She whirled her hand around, and the ghost went flying. It hit one of the walls and slid down.

Slid down?

Helaine realized with a start that the ghost hadn't passed through the wall for some reason. It had hit it and slid down, dazed. As if it had become somehow more solid . . .

Helaine suddenly figured out what was happening. "The *tassim* drink blood to become more real!" she called to Score. "Look at them! They're becoming more solid the more they drink!" She stared at one coming for her. It now had a faint pink color, and she understood the blood was giving it that tint. It had spread throughout the ghost.

Making it more solid. And if it was solid . . .

As the *tassim* attacked her, Helaine whirled her sword and struck. It was like trying to cut milk, but at least there was some resistance. She could fight back! With a growl, she struck again.

There was a thin, reedy wail from the ghost, which jumped back from the attack. It appeared to be wounded and hurt, which was just fine with her. She herself was hurting from their bites. It was payback time. "We can slay them now," she told Score. "They're real enough to be harmed."

"Good," he said, and immediately conjured up a ball of fire, throwing it at the closest *tassim*. The ghost howled as the fire consumed it, burning away to nothing.

Helaine preferred to use her sword. She hacked at the closest ghost until it was in tiny, quivering pieces that promptly vanished.

Two down, four to go.

The *tassim* obviously realized that they were in trouble, but they could still smell blood. Their thirst overcame their fear, and all four attacked together. Helaine took on two with her sword. One managed to bite her arm as she chopped the other to shreds. Then she slammed the ghost attacking her into the wall, dazing it as she lopped off its head.

The pieces of both ghosts vanished like evaporating dew.

Score had figured out a different way to take on his two attackers. With his chrysolite gem, he had control over Water, and blood was mostly water. Concentrating, he froze the water within the ghosts. This made them transparently solid and immobile. Picking each one up, he slammed them against each other. They both shattered into shards of ice that melted away.

Panting, Helaine resheathed her sword. "Good work," she complimented him.

"Thanks," he said. "I'm glad you figured out what was happening. And, boy, are you a mess."

Helaine looked at herself. She had several wounds on each arm, one on her leg, and one on her ankle. Blood was trickling from them, and they all ached. "We really have to figure out some sort of a healing spell," she said. He had just as many bloody tracks on his skin. "And we could do with dressing these wounds before we slowly bleed to death. But there's no water or bandages."

"Water I can supply," he told her, holding up his gem. "There's plenty of it in the air, since you need it to make mist and fog. Bandages are a little harder to come by."

"My turn, I suppose," Helaine said. Using the knife from her boot, she chopped the bottom nine inches or so off her tunic. This left it at about waist-length, short enough to make her uncomfortable. At least she still had her chain mail over it, so she wasn't indecent. She chopped the cloth into lengths, and

Score immediately soaked them all. They took turns patching each other up, though Helaine retreated to another room to dress her thigh. When she returned, Score gave a gentle laugh.

"Well, we both look quite silly," he told her. Helaine glanced down at herself, and then at him with bandages all over, and had to agree.

"But it's better than bleeding to death," she pointed out. "The wounds should seal themselves up pretty quickly, and then we can dump the bandages."

"Maybe we'd better hang on to them," Score said. "This place is getting pretty violent. Anyway, we'd better get on with the search, don't you think?"

"Yes." She gestured across the courtyard. "Stables next, I suppose. Come on."

"Well, there's one good thing about the castle being run-down," Score said, falling in beside her. "At least there won't be any fresh horse droppings."

Helaine chuckled at that. Score was no animal lover, that was for certain. She, on the other hand, would have liked little better than to have a horse right now. Or, better still, Flame, her unicorn friend from Dondar. Helaine loved to ride, and putting up with a little smell was worth the advantages.

They checked out the stables, which were as ruined as the rest of the castle, and then moved on to the blacksmith's shop. The anvil, being solid iron, was still there, as were some parts of the tools such as hammer heads. But still there was no sign of life.

"Kitchens next," Score said, and winced. "I wish that didn't remind me of how hungry I am. All I need is a simple living thing to morph into food. . . ."

"You're always thinking of your stomach," Helaine answered. "You must be related to Blink."

"And you're not hungry?" he asked her.

"Of course I am," she replied. "But a warrior learns to endure adversity without complaining about it. You should try it some time."

"I'm not a warrior," he answered. "I'm a wimp."

"You're no wimp," she answered firmly.

That seemed to embarrass him. "Okay, an ex-wimp, then. But I'm still hungry. We'd better find Pixel and defeat Destiny soon, or you're going to be complaining about how loudly my stomach's growling."

Helaine just snorted, and led the way into the broken-down kitchen. The room was large, and mostly empty. The far wall was a large fireplace, with a built-in oven for baking bread. Some of the metalwork in the fireplace remained intact, including the spit for rotating cooking meat. But, once again, there was no sign of life.

"I'd call this a wild goose chase," Score commented. "Except there aren't even any geese. Pixel's not here, is he?"

"No," Helaine agreed reluctantly. "And there's no sign that he ever was, either." She shook her head. "When we were attacked here, I was *sure* he was around. Why else would Destiny attack us here?"

"Maybe Destiny isn't the one attacking us," Score suggested. "Don't forget — according to Shanara, nobody ever comes back from this planet. I think there's a home-grown menace after us that has nothing to do with Destiny."

Helaine considered his point. "You may be right," she agreed. "But how could anything like that create my father's castle here?"

"From your imagination somehow," Score said. "After all, those *tassim* were from a story you knew; certainly they're nothing like anything I've heard of before. I have a strange suspicion that whatever it is that rules this planet can read minds. And it's picked yours to work from."

"What a lovely thought," Helaine replied. "If only it had picked some of the nicer thoughts."

"You're hardly ever nice," Score told her. "It probably couldn't find any nice thoughts." Then he pretended to cringe from an imaginary blow.

Helaine grimaced, but wasn't upset. She knew that Score was only joking with her, as he always did. "Well, let's get out of here," she said, "and continue the search. I for one won't be sorry to leave this place behind. It's like meeting the corpse of an old and dear friend — very unsettling."

"I can imagine," Score said dryly. "Well, let's just hope that our unseen foe hasn't lifted any more ideas from your imagination. Just how many nasty stories do you know, anyway?"

"Lots, unfortunately," Helaine admitted. The ground shook beneath their feet as it had since they'd arrived on the planet. But this time . . .

"Is it just my imagination," she asked, "or was that tremor stronger than the rest?"

It came again, almost knocking them off their feet.

"Earthquake!" yelled Score, looking around for safer ground. They were almost beneath the main gateway now, and the ground shook again. But there was something odd about it.

"I don't think it's an earthquake!" Helaine exclaimed. "It's only this part of the castle that's being affected." The far end of the castle seemed perfectly normal. It was only the area around the gate that was shaking.

"This is weird," Score complained, striving to keep his balance. "What could be causing it?"

"Offhand, I'd say *that*," Helaine answered, pointing through the gateway.

The ground had burst open in the moat, and a huge skeleton had reared up. It had once clearly been some kind of immense snake. Now, though, it was only discolored bones. The huge head reared back, and she could see the long, sharp, poison fangs. The poison couldn't have survived, of course, but the fangs were bigger than she was. If one of them hit her, she'd be speared clean through.

The snake struck forward, its skull slamming into the portcullis. The weakened metal shattered and collapsed, but the strike slowed the snake for a moment. Helaine and Score dived aside as the skull struck out at them again. Helaine rolled and was quickly on her feet, sword in hand, ready to meet this new foe.

It couldn't hiss at her, since it had no voice, but it *could* dart forward at lightning speed, the two immense fangs driving down at her. Helaine managed to parry the closest, but the strength of the blow knocked her off her feet. Dazed, she watched it rear to strike at her again.

Then a fireball exploded in its face, and Score yelled, "Hey, what about me, you jerk?" He danced around, waving his arms at the creature. The snake-thing reared back and struck out at him. Helaine realized that Score was distracting it, giving her time to recover from the blow. He really was a lot braver than he believed himself to be. The snake missed its thrust as Score dodged into the blacksmith's shop. The snake's head was too large to get through the doorway, and Score stood there jeering at it.

Furious, the snake slammed its skull into the opening.

The walls cracked, and Helaine could hear stones falling inside. Score's mocking laughter ceased abruptly as he realized he was in serious trouble. There was no other way out of the building — except past the snake.

Helaine struggled to her feet, shaking off her feelings of lethargy and weariness. She had to help him somehow. But how? Unlike how she had handled the skeletons from the graveyard, she'd never be able to hack this snake apart. Its bones were simply too massive and strong for that.

What she needed was a plan.

What she needed was to forget her sword for now. She had to remember that she wasn't just a warrior, she was also a magic-user. This was a situation in which her gems would be handier than her sword. Her agate for communications was no use. The snake wasn't really alive, just reanimated, so there was no talking to it. Onyx? That gave her the power to change her own shape. But what could she change into that might be able to fight a giant snake? She didn't have a clue. That left her sapphire, for levitation, and her chrysoprase, for control over the element of Earth.

Or, maybe, *both* together . . .

She had the barest outline of a plan now. The first thing she had to do was to get the snake to go after her instead of Score. That was the dangerous part. It was still head-butting the blacksmith's shop, and the walls were on the verge of collapse.

"Over here!" she yelled, clutching a gemstone in each fist. Using the chrysoprase, she made a wall rear up out of the earth between the snake and Score, and then concentrated her powers on the stones lying around the yard. They were heavy, but with concentration she could move them. Picking one up mentally, she flung it at the skeletal snake with all of her strength.

It hit one of the creature's ribs, shattering the bone instantly. This got the snake's attention. It whirled away from Score and sprang back at her.

Helaine dived into the doorway of the Great Hall. This one was large enough for the snake to pass through, too.

"No!" Score yelled. "It can follow you!"

Which was, of course, what she wanted. The snake thrust its head through the arched doorway, looking to see where she had gone.

Helaine focused her powers of levitation and Earth magic at the wall above it. She shook the foundations and tore the entire wall apart. With a roar it collapsed, and tons of rock rained down on the startled skeletal snake. It vanished under the rock and debris.

Dust made her gasp and choke as the wall tumbled down. Using her gems, she made certain that none of the stones came anywhere near her. But the collapse seemed to go on and on. The Great Hall was crumbling to pieces all around her. Coughing and choking, she had to wait for the rock rain to cease.

Finally, there was peace once more. Helaine's eyes were streaming because of the dust, but she could make out the shattered snake bones beneath the ancient rocks. As she'd hoped, even the snake couldn't withstand a couple of tons of rock being dumped on it. The bones had snapped and died again.

Score hurried through the cloud of dust. "Helaine!" he yelled frantically. "You idiot! Be alive!"

"I am," she managed to say, between coughs. "Just."

"You crazy fool," he snapped angrily. "Whatever made you do a dumb trick like that?"

"Trying to save your life," she answered. "And it may have been dumb, but it worked." She pointed to the remains of the snake.

"You could have killed yourself," Score said, his expression halfway between relief and anger.

"But I didn't," Helaine pointed out. She was able to talk without coughing now. "So a *thank-you* would seem to be appropriate."

Score collapsed onto a convenient stone. "Thank you," he said. "But don't scare me like that again."

She raised an eyebrow. "Why, you'd almost think you *cared* about me."

"Well, don't start thinking that," he ordered. "It's just that I don't have many friends, and I don't want to lose one. Even the one who's a pain."

"Ah." Helaine nodded, pretending that she believed the excuse. For some reason, Score seemed to think that caring about other people was a weakness. Well, he'd learn. "So, are you going to sit around all day, or shall we get moving?" She put her crystals back into her pouch, and wiped some of the dust from her face. "While we still can," she added.

Score was exhausted, she could see. It took all his willpower to get back on his feet. He sighed and stared at her. "Well, all I can say is that you have a very active imagination. Can we get out of here before another one of your nightmares comes after us?"

"It might be wisest," she agreed. She was bone-weary, too, and her body protested as she started back toward the gateway. Score limped along beside her, not looking at her. He seemed to be embarrassed by his earlier concern. Helaine was quite touched. But now was not the time to discuss it. "You know what's happening, don't you?" she asked him. "I don't think that these attacks are aimed at killing us."

"If they're not," he answered with a scowl, "then somebody's got really lousy aim."

"I think they're meant to do precisely what they are doing," Helaine explained. "They're meant to tire us out. To exhaust us. So we'll collapse, unable to go on."

He got her point. "To drain us so that we have to sleep," he realized.

"Exactly." She sighed. "And, frankly, it's working. We can't keep this up for very much longer."

"But what else can we do?" he asked.

It was a good question. Unfortunately, she didn't have a good answer.

CHAPTER 6

Pixel was marching through the maze feeling quite pleased with himself. He'd managed to outwit Destiny and escape, and now all he had to do was to get out of the labyrinth. Then he could rest. For some reason, he felt pretty tired. Well, it wasn't too surprising. He'd been through a big fight on Earth saving Score's life, and then had been kidnapped and brought here. Using magic always drained his strength a little, so it was probably simply an accumulation of everything that had drained him so much.

Of course, Pixel worried that he was wrong. Maybe there was another problem that he wasn't aware of? He'd assumed that all of his problems stemmed from Destiny. But each world he'd visited so far tended to have a magician to rule it. Why would Zarathan be any exception? Maybe he was overlooking another player in this game.

Well, he would soon see about that. He took out his ruby again and concentrated. He needed to find out where the greatest threat to his life came from. He focused on the problem, and waited for some kind of an answer.

Nothing happened.

Was something interfering with his powers? He concentrated on finding the nearest exit, and a red light shone out, showing him the door he'd seen earlier. So if that worked, why couldn't he find out where his greatest threat was coming from?

Disturbed and confused, he replaced the gemstone and continued walking. When he came to a T-junction, he took the left-hand path.

And then he stopped.

Just ahead of him was a small table set against the wall. There was nothing on it, and there was no apparent reason for it to be there. He studied it, but it appeared to be a simple table, with four legs. There was a gash in the top of it that looked like someone had struck it with a sword. Other than that, it was perfectly ordinary. Still, this was the first piece of furniture he'd seen in the maze outside the central room. Pixel shrugged and went on.

He soon came to a crossroad in the passages, and used his ruby to discover the way out was straight on. Then he had to turn left and left again. Then right, and then two more lefts. Pixel had a good memory, but it was hard for him to picture this pathway in his mind. Somehow, he couldn't get it to work out straight. Maybe it was because he was so tired. . . .

He turned the next corner and saw another table in front of him. It looked just like the one he'd seen earlier, and had to be its twin. Perhaps there had been a reason once why they were placed here. He was about to walk past it when he saw that it had a gash in it, exactly like the other one had.

Exactly.

Pixel stared at the table, and wondered if he was leaping to the wrong conclusion. Just because this table looked exactly like the other didn't mean it *was* the other. Only that it was possible . . . but if it *was* the same table, he must have walked in a circle, and that wasn't right. The first table had been after a T-junction. This one was in a straight passage. It *had* to be a different table.

But it looked exactly the same . . .

Then Pixel grinned. Of course! Someone had made a couple of identical tables — if not more — and scattered them throughout the maze. The idea was to make people think they were walking in circles when they really weren't. It was just a trick to discourage him. It also meant that there would most likely be other tables just like this one ahead of him. It was simple to deal with the problem. Using the ruby, he carved a large P in the surface of the wood. If he saw more tables without the P, he'd *know* they weren't the same table. Feeling pleased with his solution, he marched on again.

Ten minutes later, he saw another table ahead of him, this time next to a crossroad. Cheerfully, he strode toward it and grinned as he looked down at it.

Next to a gash in the surface was the letter P he'd carved.

Pixel felt like somebody had punched him in the stomach. He stared down in disbelief. The table *had* to be the same one. Nobody could have known he'd carve his initial in the other one and be able to do the same to this. But . . . how *could* this be the same table? It didn't make sense. It was always in a different position.

Maybe there was just the one table, then? Pixel could accept that. Did it necessarily mean he was walking in circles? No, he figured. Maybe it was some sort of magic table, and it was teleporting from place to place in the maze, so that it always appeared in front of him? That way, he could still be going in the right direction and yet it would make it look like he wasn't. That was one possibility, certainly. Now, how could he test that theory?

Using the ruby, he focused on finding the previous table he'd passed. The gemstone lit up the table in front of him with a red glow. As he'd come to suspect, it *was* the same table. Next, he focused on the *place* where it had stood before.

The floor underneath the table lit up.

Pixel shook his head. This was impossible! The same table, and it hadn't moved? But it was always in a different place! It *couldn't* be the same table in the same spot when the spot itself was different.

Pixel knew he had to think logically. He'd always believed that anything could be solved if he simply applied his mind to it. He just had to concentrate and follow the train of thought to the proper end. There was only one table, and the ruby insisted it stayed in one spot. But the walls looked different each time he saw the table. If the table stayed constant . . .

The *walls* had to be different.

Somehow, the walls were changing. They looked solid, as far as he could see, but that didn't mean too much. Was it possible that they could be moving somehow, and altering the path of the maze? There was a simple way to test that. He'd come on the table after making a right-hand turn. All he had to do was to retrace his steps by going back around what would now be a left-hand bend.

He turned around, and saw that there was indeed something very wrong. There wasn't a left-hand turn. Or a right-hand turn.

The walls *were* changing. The way he'd come had sealed up and a new way back opened.

Pixel was starting to get really worried now. If the labyrinth was changing on him, then it meant he wasn't actually going anywhere, no matter how hard he might try. The pathways were constantly altering, so he was in fact going around in circles. Even though there was an exit door, he'd never be allowed to reach it.

And now he knew why the table had been placed there. It was to prove to him that he was trapped. That there was absolutely no way out of the maze. That he could try forever and still get nowhere, because the maze would shift to keep him imprisoned.

Whoever had built the maze had cheated. This wasn't something people were meant to ever escape from. It was Pixel's worst nightmare — a logical puzzle that had no answer because it wasn't constructed fairly.

Discouraged, he sat down on the table. It creaked a bit, but supported his weight. This was crazy. He could never find a way out of this. Well, not now, anyway. There had to be a solution, but the problem was that he was too tired to think as clearly as normal. He needed a short rest, and he'd be better.

Then he heard a noise.

Puzzled, he listened. Had he been imagining it?

No. He heard it again. It was a clacking sound, coming from a distance. The trouble was, the corridors conducted the sound, making it echo and re-echo, so he couldn't decide where it was actually coming from. But clearly he wasn't alone in the maze. It didn't sound like it was any kind of noise that Destiny would be making, so presumably it was something else. Maybe she'd sent something after him once she'd discovered him missing.

Maybe she didn't know the nature of this maze, either. He'd been wondering why she hadn't come after him. Now, maybe, he knew the answer: With the maze constantly shifting, she could be hunting for him and even be very close without ever actually finding him.

The clicking sound was getting louder. Pixel still couldn't tell where it was coming from, but the thing had to be closer. Would it be able to find him, whatever it was?

Pixel knew his safest option would be to start moving again, in any direction. If the walls shifted to lock him in, they'd most likely also end up locking out whatever it was that was after him. He set off down the corridors, taking the turns at random and stopping from time to time to listen.

The thing was definitely getting closer. He was pretty sure it was behind him now, and catching up. But he still didn't have any idea what it was he was fleeing. All he knew was that it had to be large. The clacking sounds must be its footsteps; judging from the number of them, the creature was probably four-footed. Beyond that, he could guess nothing. Instead, he hurried on, trying to place some distance between him and *it*.

But it was still drawing closer. He realized that it had to be moving quicker than he was, and four legs probably didn't hurt its speed. He was feeling quite tired, and badly needed a rest. He passed the table another time.

Then he heard a snort from behind him, and knew the creature had caught up with him. He whirled around, trying to think of something he could do. He stared in shock at the monster.

It was a rat. While that seemed somehow logical inside a maze, this rat had to be twenty feet long, not counting the thin tail. Its huge whiskers twitched as it stared hungrily at him with glaring red eyes. Its mouth opened, showing off razor-sharp teeth. With a squeal, it skittered forward, its claws making the clicking noise he'd been hearing for so long.

Pixel considered running, but there wasn't much point. Whoever was controlling this maze had obviously wanted the rat to catch him this time; no doubt it would be able to catch him again. In which case, he might as well stand here and fight, rather than retreat and exhaust himself further.

Focusing on the topaz, Pixel concentrated on Fire. Instantly, the table burst into flames almost directly under the monster. The rat squealed in pain and anger, retreating slightly from the flames. It snarled loudly and pawed at the table, knocking it apart. The wood was burning so intensely that the fire simply couldn't last. As the flames died down, the rat charged forward again.

Pixel tossed a fireball at it. The rat screamed again as the blazing sphere hit it, singeing its fur. But the blow simply made it angrier, and it lashed out at Pixel with a huge paw. Pixel jumped aside, but the paw caught him a glancing blow, knocking him into the wall. He was stunned for a second and the rat sensed victory. It snickered and jumped toward him.

Pixel concentrated all of his energy on the beryl. This controlled the element of Air, and he was able to solidify the air in front of him into a crystalline barrier. The rat slammed into this and squealed loudly.

This brought Pixel a moment's relief, but hardly more than that. The rat threw itself against the far side of the barrier, and there was a cracking sound. He saw spiderweb fractures run through the solid air. The rat was too strong for his plug to remain for long. It would smash its way through to him in minutes.

So he had to have another plan. Air had to be the key here, and Pixel concentrated on the beryl. He really didn't want to hurt the rat if he didn't have to. So he focused on the air on the far side of the barrier, changing the nitrogen into knockout gas.

The rat threw itself against the barrier again, and the small fissures became huge cracks. It couldn't stand up to much more of this. . . .

The rat howled out defiance and sucked in a lungful of fresh air. Or, rather, knockout gas. Even through the broken crystal, Pixel could see its face twist and its eyes go unfocused. It mewed in shock, but its next breath brought in more of the gas. The rat staggered, trying to stay upright, but it was useless. The giant creature collapsed into a heap, out to the world.

Pixel collapsed, too, in sheer relief. He'd managed to stop the monster, and he was safe for the moment. What he needed now was a way out of the maze. But it was so hard to think straight. . . . With the corridor safely blocked, Pixel figured it would be the perfect time to catch just a little sleep. The rest would refresh him, and he'd be able to go on again, able to concentrate on his problems.

Just a little nap, he promised himself. . . .

CHAPTER 7

Score was really glad to be leaving the castle behind them. The vampire ghosts, the living skeletons, and the bone snake had disturbed him almost as much as seeing her home in ruins had disturbed Helaine. She was still brooding about it, he could tell. It was something he knew he'd never understand, because he had no real attachment to a place.

Score was regretting having forced Helaine to confront the fact that she wasn't really a Votrin. He wouldn't have done it if she hadn't annoyed him so much. Sometimes she was the best friend he could ever hope for, and other times she simply drove him crazy. He imagined that all girls were like that, though he had no way of knowing. Helaine was the first one he'd ever really made friends with since Alida Lopez in second grade. And Alida had lost interest in him pretty quickly.

Well, there wasn't much point in brooding; what was done, was done. Helaine seemed to be coping with her loss in her own way, alternating being grouchy with being noble. As long as she dealt with it, that was the main thing.

"I've been thinking," Helaine announced abruptly.

"Wow," Score said. "That's a good habit. I hope you keep it up."

She glared at him. "I was thinking that all of this —" she gestured around her "— is based on my own memories and knowledge, somehow."

"So?"

"So, perhaps I can figure out the logic of it. We've passed through my home and Pixel wasn't there. Where would he be, then? Where in my thoughts would he be hidden?"

"I don't know," Score said patiently. "Where?"

"I don't know, either," Helaine admitted.

"Well, your thinking's *really* helping us out," Score complained. "Maybe you should stick to chopping things up; at least *that's* helpful."

Helaine whirled around at him. "I've had just about enough from you today," she snapped. "One moment you're being thoughtful and kind, and the next you're insulting me. Your mood swings are getting very irritating."

"And yours aren't?" he shot back. "Listen, ever since we got lost in *your* nightmares, we've had nothing but trouble. You can't expect me to be all sweetness and light after what we've been through."

She calmed down a little. "Probably not," she admitted. "But I'm getting *really* sick of your insults. It's not helping me to think."

Score realized that she was right. "I'm sorry," he said with a sigh. "I guess it's the weariness getting to me. I shouldn't be so snappy. It's not your fault that whatever it is on this planet is tapping into your subconscious and . . ." His voice trailed off as something suddenly came to him. "That's it! Helaine, you're a genius!"

"I am?" She looked amazed and pleased. "What did I do?"

"You're right about having to know something about this land and where Pixel is," he explained excitedly. "And of course you can't think out what it is. This place is tapping into your dreams, your memories — all the subconscious things in your mind. The nonlogical parts. What we have to do is to get into the same place, and then maybe we can figure out what it is you know."

"Conscious?" she asked. "Subconscious? What are you talking about."

Right; he'd forgotten she wouldn't know anything about psychology. "The mind is a complicated place," he said, trying to remember it accurately and explain it simply. "There are different sorts of things going on in there. There's the automatic stuff, like remembering to breathe, that you don't have to think about. There's the conscious stuff, which you know and can tap into, like your memory, or being able to think. And then there's the subconscious, which is all the weird stuff: dreams, nightmares, fears, all kinds of things that are halfway between conscious and automatic. Like, for example, if I were to draw a sword and attack you, you'd probably counter the blow without even having to think about it. It's not automatic, but it's not something you need to focus too hard on.

"That's the part of your mind that our unknown foe has tapped into, and it's what we have to tap into, as well."

Helaine had struggled a bit to follow this, but she seemed to have grasped the main points. "I see. So, how do we tap into my dreams?"

"Well, that's the problem," Score admitted. "I should think hypnosis would work — if I knew how to do it. But if we *did* get into your dreams, would that mean that the planet could, too?"

Helaine went a little pale. "It's possible. But . . . if it's the only way to save Pixel, maybe we should try anyway."

"No," Score snapped. "I wouldn't want to lose both of you. But maybe there's some other way to do it? How about in your book of spells? Does that have anything that might be able to get into your hidden thoughts?"

Helaine shrugged, and then pulled the book out. She kept intending to go through it and make an index to the spells, but somehow she never seemed to have the time. She knew where several of the most important were, but there were others she still hadn't figured out. She flicked through the book as they walked, trying to decide from the headings if any of the spells might be useful. Finally, she came to one which said: FOR GUIDANCE FROM THE SOUL. "This might be it," she said. "Only —"

"— it's in code, as usual," Score said with a sigh. "Okay, let's see if we can solve this without Pixel's help."

SE YUR NAE TIMS TIMS TIMS MINU HE TIRD AN HE FFTH

86

"Se yur nae?" Score said aloud. "What is *that* supposed to mean?"

"I'm not sure," Helaine replied. "And what about the three tims? What is a tim?"

"It's a nickname for Timothy."

"A nickname?"

Score sighed. He wished he could give Helaine an earthling dictionary, so he wouldn't have to always explain things.

"A nickname," he told her, "is a name you are given instead of your real name. Like Score's my nickname. Most nicknames are abbreviations of the real names — basically the same names with some letters lopped off. So Timothy would be Tim. Pixel would be Pix. And you would be —"

"I got it!" Helaine suddenly cried. "You're absolutely right."

"Of course I am. About what?"

"That's the key to the code. The letters are cut off. Look at the word *yur*. It must be *your* without the *o*. And *ffth* must be *fifth*."

"The first word could be *see*," Score volunteered.

"Or *use*. If *your* is missing its second letter, the first word is probably missing its first."

Slowly, Score and Helaine decoded the rest of the message.

87

"Use your name times times times minus the third and the fifth," Helaine recited slowly. "But why are there three times?"

Score thought about it for a moment. "Probably because you have to use your name three times," he formulated.

"Minus the third and the fifth letters," Helaine concluded.

"Okay," Score said, happily. "It's nice to see we can manage a puzzle ourselves. Let's do it."

Helaine nodded and together they focused on the spell. Since it was Helaine's dreams they needed to access, she said the word aloud — *Heane* — while Score simply thought it. He could feel the magic flowing, but saw absolutely nothing. Apparently, though, Helaine could see perfectly. She went pale, and then shook her head.

"That's not it," she said firmly.

"How do you know?" Score asked her. "Maybe it's something you need to talk over?"

"That's *not* it," Helaine repeated, almost angrily. "The spell must have found . . . something else I was worrying about. I guess I wasn't focused enough. Let's try again."

"Okay," Score said, wondering what she could have seen that would have bothered her so much that she didn't want to talk about it. Oh, well, it was probably a girl thing and nothing for him to worry about. They repeated the spell, and this time Helaine nodded.

"This is it," she said grimly. "I know how we can find Pixel now."

"Well, that's great," Score said enthusiastically. Then he saw Helaine's face, and asked: "Isn't it?"

"Not really," she replied. "We have to ask the Fair Folk."

"The Fair Folk?" Score was lost. "Who are they?"

"Don't you have those legends on your world, either?" Helaine gestured. "Let's start walking, and I'll explain as we go along." She set off, and he fell into step beside her. "In our myths, the Fair Folk were the race who lived on Ordin before mankind. They were magical creatures of air and mystery, and lived in a strange sort of harmony with nature. When men came, they were cold and hard and brutal, and took the land that really belonged to the Fair Folk. The Fair Folk tried to fight, but they couldn't stand up against cold steel and the anger of human beings. As a result, they were forced to retreat from our world deep underground. There they live, still furious with humans for taking their land. Sometimes people find a way into the world of the Fair Folk. Many of those never return. Some, however, return and discover that many years have passed."

"I've heard stories like that," Score admitted. "Rip Van Winkle . . . We call them fairies, mostly, and they're supposed to be cute little things a few inches high, with butterfly wings and pixie dust."

"They can't be the same as our Fair Folk, then," Helaine decided. "Ours are human-sized, and intensely magical. I used to think that they were just stories, but . . . well, after all we've been through, maybe they weren't."

Score scowled. "You're thinking that they must have been magic-users, aren't you? But if they *were*, they couldn't have been very powerful. After all, Ordin's right on the outside of the Diadem, like Earth, and magic doesn't work too well there."

"Not for *humans*," she agreed soberly. "But perhaps the Fair Folk were much stronger than humans with magic. And maybe they really do still exist."

Score shivered at the thought. "Well, either way, it doesn't make much difference. The Fair Folk we find here are going to be the ones from your dreams, not the real things. So, how bad can they be if you call them *fair*? Surely they'll be decent to us?"

"It's not that kind of fair," Helaine said. "They are called 'fair' because they have light features. They don't like humans, and they'd just as soon kill you as say hello."

"If it's all the same to them, I know which option I'd prefer," Score said. "Have you noticed that there's a common thread running through the Diadem? Nobody seems to like human beings very much."

Helaine shrugged. "Given the nasty disposition of the average magician, who can blame them?"

"I'm not exactly blaming them," Score answered. "I just wish they'd all learn the idea that everyone's innocent until proven guilty."

"Huh." Helaine snorted. "In these worlds, it's safer to assume that people are guilty until proven innocent."

"For *them*, maybe. Not for *us*." Score sighed. "So, we're looking for a bunch of people who don't like us at all. Is there any other cheerful news that you've got for me?"

"Yes." Helaine's face was very grim. "You're not going to like the way we have to enter their realm." She gestured ahead of them.

"Why am I not surprised?" Score asked. "You *always* seem to be able to make a bad situation worse." He studied the object she had pointed at. It looked like a long, low hill at first. Then he realized that it was far too regular to be natural. "What *is* that?"

"It's a barrow," she replied. She didn't look happy.

"Where are its wheels?" he asked, trying to lighten up the mood.

"It's not that kind of a barrow," Helaine said seriously. "It's a burial mound for a warrior. In the old days on my world, all brave chieftains were buried in those."

"It's a *grave*?" Score realized, chilled again. "These Fair Folk live in a *grave*? Couldn't they find a nice condominium?"

Helaine sighed. "They don't live *in* the grave, they live *under* it," she informed him. "I told you, they live underground, to avoid humans. And what better way to keep humans out than to make the entrance to their world in a human grave?"

"Well, their logic is impeccable," Score said. "It's going to keep me out. I don't dig graves." He managed a thin smile. "That's sort of a joke," he explained. "Dig . . . graves . . ."

She ignored him. "We have to go through their entrance. It's the only way to find Pixel."

Ouch! Score eyed the barrow with trepidation and then sighed deeply. "He's going to owe me major for this one, you know." He glared at her in sudden suspicion. "Are you *sure* there isn't an easier way to contact them? You're not doing this just to spook me, are you?"

"The only other way I've heard of," she answered, "involves tearing living hearts out of bodies. And since you're the only body . . ."

"We'll go in via the grave," Score agreed hastily. He wasn't sure whether this explanation was true, or whether it was just her idea of a joke. It *had* made her smile slightly, but that could just be cruelty. Still, knowing Helaine, it could be the truth. The grave seemed like the safer option. "So, do we need a shovel?"

"No, it's a lot simpler than that," Helaine answered. She led the way to the far end of the small hill, and he saw that there was a kind of doorway there. It was very simple, just two vertical stones and a horizontal one laid across them. A large stone filled in the space. "There's the door."

"We're supposed to move *that*?" Score asked incredulously. "It must weigh a couple of tons. Even with your levitation, I doubt we could shift it."

"No, *we* don't move it," Helaine answered. "The occupant of the barrow does."

"Occupant?" Score felt nervous again. "Uh, the occupant is *dead.*"

"Right." Helaine smiled grimly. "So he's not likely to be in a very good mood. Maybe you had better stand back a bit." She took her sword out and rapped loudly on the stone with its hilt. "Whoever lies in here," she cried out as loudly as she could, "come forth!"

This was looking like a worse and worse idea all the time to Score. Looking for the Fair Folk was bad enough, but raising the dead to get there. . . . No way did he want to be a part of this. Unfortunately, he didn't have a choice.

For a moment, nothing happened, and Score was almost ready to breathe a sigh of relief and try and figure out some other way to find Pixel.

Then he heard a loud groan from inside the barrow. A moment later, with a terrible creaking sound, the rock that blocked the entrance swung aside. Score stared in horror at the figure that slowly emerged into the insipid moonlight.

It was a giant, almost eight feet tall and built in proportion. Helaine wasn't a small girl, being about five foot ten, but she was dwarfed by this creature. He was dressed in faded armor like hers, only his chain mail looked a lot heavier and stronger. He wore a metal cap with a noseguard, and had a thick reddish beard. In one way, he was sort of a relief, because he didn't look like he'd been dead for very long. His flesh and skin seemed to be pretty intact.

There was, however, a kind of sickly greenish color to his skin that made Score queasy. It was probably lucky that he hadn't managed to find anything to eat. And the big guy had a stench of decay about him, too.

"Who dares to challenge me?" the giant asked. His voice was deep and echoing, with a rattle of the grave added to it. Score shuddered.

Helaine stood up as tall as she could and raised her sword. It almost reached up to his nose. "I do. I am Helaine, daughter of the House of Votrin."

The giant stared down at her in astonishment, and then managed a laugh. "A *girl*?" he asked. "A girl comes to challenge me?" He obviously found the thought to be very amusing.

"Perhaps," Helaine said, scornfully. "*If* you're worth my time. You haven't bothered to tell me *your* name, so it's obviously one you're not very proud of. In that case —" She started to shrug, as if she didn't care.

"You are *asking* to die!" the giant howled angrily. "Know me, then, and tremble! I am Cormac the Red-handed of the House of Morn! I trust that you have heard of me?"

Helaine nodded grimly. "The stories say that you stood alone at the battle of Drine, and slew two hundred men."

"Two hundred and eight," Cormac rumbled. "They always round the figures off for legends, don't they?"

Score tried to smile, and suspected that he failed miserably. "Excuse me, your giganticship," he said nervously. "I'd like a quick word with my impetuous friend, if you wouldn't mind."

Cormac glared angrily down at him. "And who are you, boy?" he howled. "Identify yourself!"

"Uh, I'm Score, of the House of . . . Frankenstein," he replied, saying the first thing that came into his mind. "And I'm new to this slaying game. I'm really much better at running and hiding. Excuse us a second, please." He grabbed Helaine's arm and dragged her back a couple of paces. "Look, I know this is your nightmare, but have you seen the *size* of that guy? And he's killed two hundred and eight men! That's approximately two hundred and seven up on you."

"That was just in one battle," Helaine said patiently. "His grand total is up around a thousand, I think."

"Whatever," Score said, gesturing wildly with his hands. "My point is that you've got to be *crazy* getting him worked up like this. Why don't we try and flatter him, and then get him to let us into his tomb once we're all friends?"

"It doesn't work like that," Helaine replied. "The only way into his grave is to defeat him in battle. We *have* to fight him, or we can't go in."

Score gave a nervous laugh. "If it's all the same to you, I'm way willing to look for an alternate route."

"The heart-donating scenario?" asked Helaine sweetly.

"I'm being suckered here, I know it." Score threw his hands up in disgust. "What makes you think you can defeat *him*?"

"I can't," Helaine answered patiently. "We *both* have to do it, otherwise we can't both enter the grave."

"Oh, we'll enter the grave all right," Score said helplessly. "The next guy to come along and knock on the door is going to find three bodies inside it." He glared at her. "If you'd told me this was part of the deal upfront, I'd never have agreed to it."

"That's why I didn't tell you upfront," Helaine answered. She turned back to Cormac. "The two of us against you," she called. "*If* you think you stand a chance."

"A chance?" Cormac howled. He drew a sword that was even larger that Score was tall. "Prepare to die!"

Score decided that he was *not* prepared — but that he was likely to die anyway. . . .

CHAPTER 8

Helaine considered attempting to block the wild swing that Cormac had aimed at her, but then realized if she did, the impact would probably break her arms. Instead, she ducked low under the blow and hacked backhand at his arm as it flashed past. Her sword bit into his muscle, and he roared.

A thin greenish liquid splashed out instead of blood. Cormac had been dead too long to have any of that left.

If the wound hurt him at all, it certainly didn't slow him down. He whirled his sword around and struck at her. This time, she had no option but to block.

The force of the blow almost drove her to her knees. Her arms ached as the two swords clanged and sprayed sparks. Her muscles felt as if they were on fire after this blow, and she could barely feel her fingers. This wasn't good; she'd have trouble attacking him like this. And they *had* to defeat him in order to continue.

"Score!" she yelled. "Do something!"

"Is fainting an option?" he asked, dodging around, trying not to attract Cormac's attention.

"Something constructive!" Helaine snarled.

"Hey, this whole thing is *your* idea!" he exclaimed. "Why do I have to be the one to get us out of it?"

Helaine didn't have time to argue with him. Cormac lumbered forward to attack again. Growling loudly, he stepped forward, his sword ready to impale her.

But his foot didn't connect with the ground. There was no ground to connect with, just a hip-deep pit. Cormac yelped and stumbled, crashing into the dirt. Helaine realized that Score had used his emerald, which gave him the power to transmute things. He must have changed the earth to gas, leaving the pit.

This gave Helaine an opening. As Cormac levered himself upright, she danced in and swung with all of her might. Her sword slashed into his forearm, almost severing it.

Then he backhanded her with his other hand, sending her flying. He collapsed again, unable to support himself as Helaine spiraled from the blow. Still, she had the presence of mind to grab hold of her chrysoprase. With control over Earth, she made the ground slam together to encase Cormac's leg in the earth.

The giant howled at this, probably more from the indignity than from any real pain. He was, after all, dead, and therefore couldn't really be feeling pain. Still, he was nicely stuck for the moment, unless he could shake himself free. Helaine staggered to her feet, looking for her sword, which she'd dropped. Then she shook her head. There was no way she was going to be able to fight Cormac with a sword. She had to use magic instead. Fishing in her bag, she pulled out her sapphire, which gave her levitation.

Meanwhile, Score was still busy. He had out his amethyst. That gave him the ability to change the size of something. She saw him concentrate, and Cormac's immense sword began to shrink.

Cormac must have realized what was going on, because he snarled and threw the sword directly at Score as hard as he could. Score almost fainted, which wouldn't have helped because the sword still would have hit him. It wasn't shrinking fast enough to be harmless when it reached him.

Helaine reached out with her powers, pushing Cormac's sword aside using levitation and throwing it to the ground several yards away. Score started breathing again. He was sweating madly, undoubtedly from pure fear. But he wouldn't give up the fight, and Helaine had to admire him for that. It was one thing to fight because you were brave; it was a lot harder to stand and fight when you really wanted to run and hide.

Cormac roared with rage again, shaking the ground to get his foot free. Helaine didn't know what to try next, especially since he seemed to be on the verge of freeing himself. Score turned to her, his face filled with worry.

"I tried transforming the air around him into knockout gas," he called. "But it didn't help."

"Of course not," Helaine snapped. "He only breathes to talk and yell. He's *dead*. The gas can't knock him out."

"Well, there goes my next idea of trying to drown him, too," Score complained. "How do you kill a guy who's already dead?"

"There's only one way," Helaine said, remembering her stories. She snatched up her sword and ran forward. "You cut off his head!" She sprang at the giant, whirling her weapon around before striking.

Cormac had raised his head to look up and curse at her. Her blow slashed into his neck, and then through. His howl of rage ceased as his head went flying from his body. It rolled several times before coming to a rest upside down, the eyes still glaring at her. Greenish goo sprayed all over her, a stinking, foul mess.

Cormac's body crumpled forward.

"Yech!" Score said, careful not to stand too close to her. "I don't like your taste in perfume."

Helaine glared at him. "If you don't shut up," she growled, "I'm going to vomit all over you." The stench was indeed making her stomach queasy.

"Hang on," Score advised her. Pulling out his chrysolite, he focused his energies. The next second, it was raining all over her. In moments, the icky green gunge had been completely washed off her, and she could breathe normally again.

"That's enough," she called. "I'm clean."

"Aw, I was just starting to have fun," Score complained. "Your hair's a real mess."

Helaine pulled some of it to where she could see it. Though the goo was gone, her hair had darkened because it was wet and looked like rats' tails hanging from her head. "I suppose I ought to thank you," she growled ungraciously.

"If you'll just wait a minute," he said, concentrating again.

Suddenly, she was perfectly dry. He'd used his gem power again to remove the water from her clothing and hair.

Her hair immediately frizzed out uncontrollably.

"Sorry," he said. "Nothing I can do about that." He tried to hide his grin at the way she looked.

Helaine closed her eyes and slowly counted to ten. She had to remind herself that she *liked* Score, and that killing him would probably not be a wise move. Then she opened her eyes again. She could feel the mess her hair was, and it annoyed her. "Come on," she growled. "I think we've earned the right to go into the tomb."

"Indeed you have," said Cormac's head.

Score looked at it and swallowed. "It's impossible to shut some people up, isn't it?"

"Magic," Helaine reminded him. The head might be disembodied, but that didn't mean it couldn't talk.

"Go through the doorway," the head advised. "There are two passages. Take the left one, vanquishers of Cormac of the House of Morn."

"Thank you," Helaine said politely. She raised her sword. "I salute your valor and your strength, Cormac the Red-handed!"

"Aren't you overdoing this politeness a bit?" Score demanded. "He's dead and apparently feeling chatty. I'm not. Let's just get on with this, shall we?"

"He was a valiant foe," Helaine protested. "He deserves recognition."

"He was *dead* to start with and even deader now," Score snapped. "If it's all the same to you, let's get on with this before my nerve snaps entirely, okay?"

Helaine could see that he was really bothered about all this. She shrugged. "As you wish." She led the way into the barrow.

There was a passageway leading down into the earth, sloping gently. Ahead, she could see the branching that Cormac had mentioned. There was the musty smell of soil all around them, and the tang of death as well. Helaine moved to take the left-hand passageway, but Score grabbed her arm.

"Whoa!" he said urgently. "What do you think you're doing?"

"Taking the passageway that Cormac mentioned," she replied, confused.

"Do you really think that's a good idea?" asked Score.

Helaine frowned. "Why would it not be?"

"Because Cormac told us to do it." He glared at her. "And, frankly, I don't see why he should be telling

104

us the truth. This is probably the wrong way, and he's sending us to our deaths."

"Why would he lie to us?" asked Helaine, not understanding.

"Maybe because we just chopped his head off?" Score suggested sarcastically. "I know if someone had done that to me, I'd be way likely to try and get my revenge."

"Ah." Helaine finally saw the problem. "Score, you can't judge Cormac by your standards. He was a brave and virtuous warrior who lived life nobly and fought and died courageously. Even dead, he would never lie, especially to someone who had bested him in a duel. We can trust his word absolutely."

Score shook his head. "It's this nobility thing again, isn't it?" he demanded. "I'm never going to get the hang of it. You're *sure* he wasn't lying?"

"Yes," she assured him. "This is my dream, after all, isn't it? I should know what the rules will be. His advice is good. If you don't trust him, trust me."

Score sighed. "I'm probably the biggest idiot in the world . . ." he muttered.

Helaine couldn't resist asking, "Only *probably*?" She turned and led the way down the left-hand passage. As she had expected, this led to the burial chamber itself. It was walled and roofed in stone, though the floor was bare earth. On the left was a raised mound, covered by a large bearskin. This was clearly where Cormac had lain until she had called him out. He had left a spear there, and a shield, resting against the side of the mount. On the right was a chariot, made from wood and leather. Unlike the other things made of wood on this world, this was still in good repair.

"His war chariot," she explained. "Once he was dead, nobody else was allowed to use it, so it was buried with him. He would need it in the fights he would face in the afterlife."

"Why am I not surprised that your myths have people fighting after they're dead?" Score asked, rolling his eyes. "You know, you have some pretty violent dreams."

"It's my culture," Helaine answered. "What do you dream about?"

"Very little to do with fighting and death," he replied. "The usual silly stuff." He looked at her. "Though I doubt you'd understand my dreams, either."

"Probably not," she agreed. "Now, there should be a clue in here as to how to deal with the Fair Folk." When he looked puzzled, she added, "That's how this sort of myth always works, so start looking."

They didn't have to look far. Score pointed to the shield. "I'd say this is it."

They both bent to examine it.

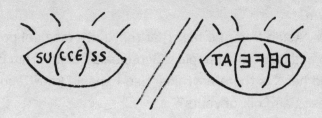

"Maybe we'll be able to figure it out later," Score suggested. He glanced around the burial chamber nervously. "Look, I really don't like this place very much, not being dead yet myself. Can we get started and see what's next?"

Helaine nodded. "Bring the shield along," she ordered. "It might come in handy. Don't worry," she added, "it's a purely defensive tool, so you should feel right at home with it."

He picked it up, and slipped his arm through the straps. "Now, how do we get to where the Fair Folk are?"

Helaine pointed to the other end of the chamber. "Through the far door," she said. "It's going to lead us downward, toward their land."

"That figures." He fell in behind her.

Crossing the chamber, Helaine walked through the far doorway. As she had suspected, there was a passageway leading downward. She snapped up a floating light to illuminate the way and started on down.

"Aside from the fact that they have magical powers and don't like people," Score said quietly from behind her, "is there anything else I should know about these Fair Folk of yours?"

"Yes," she replied, trying to recall all of the legends. "Never turn your back on them or try to run away from them. That angers them, and they'll pursue you until they kill you."

"No running away? Marvelous. There goes Plan A."

"So what's Plan B?" Helaine asked, a slight smile on her lips.

"I'll let you know just as soon as I figure it out myself," he replied. Then he shut up as they descended the passageway. Helaine realized that he was very frightened, and she couldn't really blame him. She was nervous herself. All of the dangers they had been through so far were likely to be very small compared to what might happen when they met the Fair Folk. The only reason she was going on herself was that this was their only chance of rescuing Pixel.

After about ten minutes, Helaine saw a glow ahead. She extinguished the little fireball they were following and allowed her eyes to grow used to the gloom. The light was a golden glow, permeating the tunnel ahead.

"Is that what I think it is?" asked Score nervously.

"Yes," Helaine replied. "The entrance to the realm of the Fair Folk." She gave him a reassuring smile. "Now our troubles *really* begin."

CHAPTER 9

Pixel lay against the wall, exhausted. The maze was driving him crazy. He stared at it and imagined the walls were made of bushes — bushes that were slowly grasping him . . . drowning him . . . Pixel shook his head, dispelling the hallucination. Just a little nap, and he'd be feeling much stronger again, able to tackle anything.

Provided, of course, there was nothing else in the maze with him. He glanced back at the unconscious rat, and then almost jumped.

The wall on the left of the rat opened as he watched it. It was obviously turning around a mid-point, sliding across to block the way and open up a new passage. Only it was interrupted, because the unconscious rat was blocking its path. It stuck, partly open, showing a fresh passageway behind it.

Seeing this gave Pixel the solution that he needed. He didn't have to go through the maze at all: All he had to do was to trick it! The solution made him excited enough to forget about sleep for the moment. Instead, he jumped to his feet and took the beryl out of his pocket. Control over the element of Air was just what he needed right now. The walls would switch behind him just as he walked past them, of course. But he could fix their positioning simply enough. From the ruby path, he knew the doorway that led out of the maze lay to his right, so all he had to do was to cheat and keep heading in that direction.

He walked away from the spot where he was — backward, watching the walls all the time. The wall on the left immediately spun around to block the way, and he ignored it. He didn't want to go left. As he walked further, one to the right started to open.

He immediately solidified the air into a thick rod about six feet off the ground. The wall could move no further, no matter how hard it turned. Pixel dashed back, and ran through the gap the wall had left. He was in another corridor, parallel to where he'd been, but closer to the exit. Ahead of him now was a short passage leading the way he wanted to go. When the wall started to shift, he froze the air to hold it in place and slipped through in the proper direction.

Planning carefully, Pixel made his way slowly but steadily across the maze. *This* was the way to beat it, by making it do what he wanted, not whatever its master had planned. Slowly, corridor by corridor, he worked his way across the labyrinth.

Finally, he stepped through one shifting wall to see an oak doorway right in front of him. He had made it! He'd beaten the maze! Now he would be able to get out of this place and look for his friends.

He opened the door, stepped through . . .

And was immediately disappointed. He was out of the maze, true enough, but not out of the building.

He stood in a long, narrow room made of stone that arched over his head. It had to be at least forty feet long. Down either side of the room, leaving a central walkway, were low tables. And on the tables were dozens of computers. He stared at them in amazement. On each side of the room there had to be at least fifty computers, all on and whirring quietly away to themselves. Nobody was in the room to tend them. Pixel had no idea what was going on. It seemed awfully high-tech for this particular planet.

On the other hand, perhaps these computers were linked to whatever had been controlling the maze. He realized that he'd simply assumed this world was primitive; he could easily be wrong about that.

He crossed to the first computer screen, and looked at the image.

It was very simple. It read: C:/NAME?

Pixel ignored it, and started to move on to take a look at the next one.

As he did so, the computer's mouse leaped at him from its pad with an electronic snarl. Its two buttons flared up like ears, and the thing actually *bit* him. Instead of drawing blood, it delivered a nasty electrical shock. Pixel jumped back, startled.

The screen now read: C:/NAME!

Worried, Pixel stared at the screen. It didn't seem to want to let him pass! Somehow, it knew he was out there, and it was determined to make him pay attention. But he didn't need the distraction. He inched his way forward again and the mouse hissed and reared up, ready to spring at him.

Biting his lip, Pixel leaned forward and tapped: PIXEL [ENTER].

The screen changed, showing a big smiley face. HELLO, PIXEL, it printed. LET'S BE FRIENDS.

Oh, great. A lonely computer. "Let's not," muttered Pixel. The mouse immediately jumped at him again, ready to bite him. Obviously the computer could somehow hear him. Using his beryl, Pixel made a shield in the air between him and the mouse, and dashed past the computer.

The next one whirled on its base to face him. YOU CAN'T GET PAST US ALL, it warned him. Pixel saw that the other computers in the room had also come to life. They were all moving restlessly, wires snapping, cables jiggling, mouses stomping around. There were several printers that sprang to life, firing out paper. As these emerged, they turned into paper airplanes, flying toward him. He had to duck to avoid being hit by them.

MAKE THE MOST OF IT, the computer advised him. STAY HERE AND PLAY WITH US. YOU'LL LOVE IT.

"No, I won't," Pixel muttered. "I left home to get away from computers. You must be crazy if you think I'm going to stay here with all of you."

YOU HAVE NO CHOICE, the computer said. WE CAN MAKE YOU STAY, WHETHER YOU LIKE IT OR NOT.

Pixel was starting to get worried now. There had to be at least a hundred computers in the room, all imbued with some sort of intelligence. They didn't like his refusal to stay and play, and were quite obviously getting angry about it. He could hear electronic mutterings from all over the room. The printers were snapping their feed trays open and closed. The modems were buzzing nastily, and the scanners were casting thin, intense lights across the room.

Pixel realized that this was, of course, another trap to stop him from leaving. He was being forced to stay here and keep the computers amused. They were intelligent to a degree, but they still needed a human operator to guide them. And *he* was supposed to be that operator.

"Sorry," he said. "I've got a prior engagement with my life."

The computers hissed at him. One displayed a very good likeness of him on its screen. He was hanging from a noose in some sort of electronic game of Hangman. That was clearly meant as a warning. Several were flashing red screens with DANGER!!! on them. The machines were starting to get very nasty.

Pixel couldn't allow that to dissuade him. He *had* to get out of there. This was just going to slow him down, if not actually imprison him. Grimly, he took a deep breath and started to run toward the door at the end of the room.

He didn't get far.

Cables whipped across the floor, sliding between his legs and tripping him up. Pixel went down, bruising his leg and hurting his hand as he hit the cold stone floor. The cables writhed around him, trapping his legs so that he couldn't escape. He glanced up at the closest computer screen.

THERE'S NO NEED FOR US TO BE ROUGH, it told him. JUST AGREE TO USE US. AND WE'LL LET YOU UP.

"No way," Pixel muttered.

WE HAVE WAYS TO COMPEL YOU, the screen warned him. PLEASE DON'T FORCE US TO DO IT.

They were really threatening him now. But he couldn't afford to give in. There had to be a way for him to be able to escape from this room. He just had to think of it.

DON'T BE FOOLISH, the computer warned him. WE'RE WAY SMARTER THAN YOU ARE.

"Then what do you want me for?" he yelled.

TO SHOW US WHAT TO DO, the computer answered. TO HELP US TO WORK AND PLAY. YOU MUST STAY HERE AND GIVE US PURPOSE.

"I already have a purpose," he answered. "It's to get off this world and back to my own! *Let me go!*"

YOU ASKED FOR IT, the computer told him.

Uh-oh . . . Pixel struggled to get free, but his legs were held fast. He tried to pry the cables free, but as soon as he unwound one, another wrapped itself in the first one's place. This wasn't the way to get out of there!

Then the computers moved. More wires and cables flew through the air at him, rearing and striking like snakes. The thinnest of these snapped at his arm, drawing blood. Pixel wrenched his arm free, leaving a streak of redness and pain.

They were *biting* him!

No, he suddenly realized with shock, that wasn't what they were doing at all. A second one leaped for his arm, striking and trying to worm its way under his skin.

They were trying to assimilate him into the computer net.

They were trying to connect him up to themselves! He suddenly saw what the idea was: They wanted him as an interface for Virtual Reality. They had intelligence, but no imagination. They needed him to help them react to the real world! They were going to try and take him over, to turn him into a living computer, a part of them!

He pulled the wire from his skin, releasing pain and blood. Even as he did, there were more wires coming for him. How long could he fight them off? He was getting weaker with each attack. And there were so many of them . . .

Pixel swiped at the next pair of attacking wires, and they tried a new strategy. Both sizzled at him, delivering a nasty bolt of electricity that stung and burned. They were going to shock him to the point where he'd stop struggling. Then they could take him over while he couldn't resist . . .

It was worse than his home world of Calomir; there he had worn a helmet most of his life and lived in Virtual Reality. He had grown to hate it, and had sought to escape from it into the real world. Here, the computers wanted to take him over, to make him a link between themselves and the real world. It would be a living nightmare for him.

But how could he get free? There was nothing he had that could fight computers like this. They were science, and all he had was magic. Another jab of an electrified wire burned his hand.

Then he had the solution! He grabbed the topaz from his pocket. This gave him power over the element of Fire. And what he needed wasn't exactly fire, but another aspect of it:

Electricity.

When the next wire tried to zap him, Pixel lashed out with his magic. He sent a red-hot bolt of electricity down the wire, a wave of really heavy voltage.

One of the computers exploded on the bench.

It worked!

Pixel targeted the next wire, and the next, and then sent electronic zaps down the cables holding his legs. All over the room, computers exploded, showering glass and burning metal everywhere. Pixel winced as shards sliced across him, opening new wounds.

But after a moment, his legs were free, and he could stand up again.

About twenty of the computers had exploded, their screens now black and shattered. The others seemed to be very disturbed. Pixel glared around the smoke-filled room.

"We can do this the easy way or the hard way," he said coldly. "Either you let me walk out of here, or else I fry the lot of you and then walk out of here." He held up his gemstone. "And you've seen that I can do it. So — make a decision."

After a moment, the closest intact computer put up a line of text: GET OUT OF HERE.

Pixel was glad to do exactly that. Slowly, watching for any sign of treachery, he walked the length of the room. Several of the mouses snarled and reared, but none of them attacked him. Printers muttered and scanners snapped on and off. But nothing tried to stop him. He reached the door at the far end, and opened it.

To his relief, he saw ground outside. He was free of the labyrinth and its traps! Quickly, he stepped through and closed the door behind him. Then he breathed a sigh of relief. He'd faced some of his greatest fears and won.

Thinking about this, Pixel stopped dead in his tracks. He *had* faced some of his greatest fears. He was such a logical person that one of his worst night-mares was to find himself in a place where logic didn't help him. And he had done that.

Then there was the threat of the computers taking him over. That had been a real fear of his. True, he'd managed to beat them, but it had been a pretty close call. He could have been absorbed into the computer net.

What were the odds that the problems he'd faced just happened by accident to be two of his greatest fears? Close to zero, he decided. It *couldn't* have been an accident. Which meant that the whole thing had somehow been planned. And it had to have been done from the moment he'd stepped onto the planet, because he'd arrived in the maze. Could Destiny be behind it? Somehow, he doubted that. She hadn't been planning on taking him along. Score had been the one she'd laid all her traps on Earth for, not him. So if Destiny was behind this, the traps should have been geared toward Score, which they weren't.

So the only possible answer was that there was someone else on this planet who was in the game, too. Somebody who could read minds and affect reality, bringing dreams and fears into the real world. In short, a very powerful magician. Destiny's powers had certainly increased since she'd come here, true, but he was sure she still wasn't this strong. There had to be someone else involved.

Or Destiny was much stronger than he thought.

It was all logical, and probably true; but did it help him to get out of here? His best plan was to put as much distance as he could between himself and this place.

The ground trembled beneath his feet. For a moment, he was afraid that it was an earthquake, but it stopped as suddenly as it had begun.

The planet looked dead, completely dead. A thick mist hung everywhere, and he couldn't see more than a dozen feet in any direction. There wasn't a blade of grass or a tree or bush to be seen. Just flat, gray earth. Behind him was a portion of a building, but he could see little more than a door and parts of a wall. He didn't have a clue what the building might actually look like. Nor did he really care, since all he wanted to do was to get away from it.

He didn't know which way might be best, but he figured that walking directly away from the door wouldn't hurt. He started off, stepping out as fast as he could. The problem was that he was getting really tired again after all that activity. The adrenaline rush from fighting the computers had kept him awake for a while, but he knew it wouldn't last. He desperately needed to lie down and rest a while.

The ground shook again. As before, it stopped almost immediately. He continued on, and felt the tremors at regular intervals. Odd. But what he was most interested in right now was sleep.

Only this wasn't the place to do it. Sleeping on the ground didn't appeal to him. He'd just keep going for a while, and hope that he came to a better place to rest soon. After a while, he realized that there didn't seem to be anything else out there at all. The ground was monotonously the same. There were no more buildings and no other signs of life.

Except . . .

Had he been imagining it, or had he really heard a noise some distance away? He stopped still and listened.

There it was again! Far off, but unmistakable. It was the sound of a dog howling.

Several dogs howling.

And then Pixel realized with a feeling of dread exactly what was happening. His worst nightmares coming true. . . . On Calomir, he'd been chased by a pack of starving dogs looking for food. He'd escaped then, thanks to Hakar the Beastial. There was no hope of that on this world.

He began to shake as he realized that the dogs were on his trail. They were going to hunt him down . . . and kill him.

CHAPTER 10

Score swallowed nervously and followed behind Helaine as she led him toward the golden light. He couldn't help feeling more and more worried about this whole business. From what she'd been saying, the Fair Folk were not people he really wanted to meet. Still, if they were the only way to find out where Pixel was, what option did he have?

The tunnel widened out, and there was a large gateway of some kind ahead. It looked as if it were made from solid gold, gleaming in the light of a thousand torches. There were images all over the huge doors and around the lintel. As Score and Helaine drew closer, he could see that the images showed tall, dignified people doing all kinds of savage things — chopping off heads, taking prisoners, cutting out hearts. It did not make him feel any better.

Two guards stood in front of the door. Both looked almost identical, and were clearly Fair Folk, from what Helaine had said. They were both over six feet tall, and almost too thin to be true. Their skin had a slightly golden sheen to it that he didn't think was reflected light from the doors. They had gold-colored eyes and pointed ears rather like Pixel's. Their hair was golden, and they both wore white knee-length tunics gathered at the waist by a golden belt. They had thick rings of gold around their necks. Their only difference was that one was male and the other female. They both pretended not to have seen him or Helaine approaching until Helaine stepped in front of them.

"Hail to the Fair Folk!" she said solemnly. Score assumed she knew what she was doing, and hung back slightly.

The female guard stared back at her for a moment before speaking. "Why does a human come here, knowing she will die?"

That didn't sound like a good start to Score, but Helaine smiled back at the guard. "None of us can say who will die and who will live," she answered.

"We can," the male said firmly. "No human who arrives here uninvited ever lives."

"Then invite us in," suggested Helaine.

The female guard snorted. "And why should we do that, rather than kill you where you stand?"

"Because it would be more polite," Helaine replied. "Also, it would save me the trouble of killing you, and it would save you the inconvenience of dying."

That amused the Fair Folk female. "As if you could!" she said scornfully.

The male guard looked at Score. "Do you think *you* could kill me?" he asked, equally mockingly.

"Probably not," Score admitted. "Then again, I don't like killing anything. Not even dumb animals." He winced as he said that, realizing that it sounded like he was calling the guard a dumb animal. He expected Helaine to be annoyed with him for botching the conversation.

Instead, she laughed. "Well said!" She looked at the guards. "So, will you invite us in, or do we have to kill you and invite ourselves in?"

The female guard drew her sword, longer and thinner than Helaine's. "You can try," she suggested with a grim smile. She had obviously been hoping for this. She stepped forward and began to try and penetrate Helaine's defense.

The male guard drew his sword and moved to face Score. "Draw your weapon," he said coldly. "And prepare your soul for death."

"Sorry, I don't carry weapons," Score answered, showing that his hands were empty. "How about a game of 'rock, scissors, paper' to the death, instead?"

"You'll die a lot faster than your friend," the Fair Folk male answered, and moved to attack Score anyway.

Score clutched his amethyst and focused. This altered the size of things, and he concentrated on the golden necklet the man wore, willing it to shrink.

It constricted immediately, choking the guard. With a gasp, he dropped his sword and fell to his knees, clawing at his throat for air. His face started to turn red. Score walked across to him and casually picked up the fallen sword. "Surrender," he suggested to the choking guard, "and I'll return the necklace to its normal size, so you can breathe again." The guard shook his head, refusing the offer. His fingers scrabbled to get a hold on the metal as it bit deep into his neck, but there was no way he could manage it. Finally, his face bright red, he collapsed forward, unconscious.

Score immediately returned the golden ornament to its former size. The unconscious guard whooped in a deep breath, and then began to breathe properly, his face gradually returning to its normal color.

Having beaten his foe, Score turned to see how Helaine was doing. "Do you need any help?" he called.

The female guard was stronger than she looked, and she attacked ferociously. Sparks were flying from the clash of her sword and Helaine's. Helaine was gradually being backed against the golden doors.

"No," she called, "I'm doing fine."

"Whatever," Score agreed. He tried to look nonchalant, leaning on the other guard's sword and holding Cormac's shield. But really he was watching the fighting like a hawk. If it looked for a second like Helaine was going to be hurt, he had the amethyst ready for a repeat spell.

Helaine was forced toward the door, parrying all the guard's blows but not striking back. That wasn't really like her, and Score realized that she had to be up to something. Finally, when she was almost touching the door, she made her move. The guard thrust for her heart and Helaine caught the blade on the edge of her own sword, twisting the attacking weapon upward. Then she sidestepped, so the guard stumbled forward. Helaine brought her sword around and slammed the hilt into the small of the guard's back, propelling her into the door.

When she hit the gold, there was a flash of light, and the woman yelped before collapsing forward in a heap. Score hurried over to Helaine.

"There's power in the door to keep out the unin-vited," she explained. "So I needed someone to trig-ger it."

"Nicely done," Score said. "However, we're still on the outside, and the doors are locked. If we can't touch them without getting zapped, what good does it do us?"

"Wait," suggested Helaine, resheathing her sword. "The discharge of power will have alerted the rest of the guards."

"The rest of the guards?" Score repeated. "Helaine, couldn't you give me *good* news for a change?"

"Actually, that is good news," Helaine answered, a mischievous smile on her face. She clearly knew something that he didn't, and was making the most of it. Well, he decided, let her have her fun; he wasn't playing along.

The two great doors swung silently open, and it was all Score could do not to gasp in amazement. Ahead of them was a vast city, built entirely under-ground inside an immense cavern. There were towers and spires, domes and huge halls stretching for miles into the cavern. Everything appeared to be con-structed of gold, sparkling in the light of thousands of glowing crystals that dotted the walls and ceiling of the cavern.

"I have to admit that you've got some imagination," he muttered to Helaine. "This place is impressive."

Several more guards stepped forward, spears at the ready. One, almost identical to all of the rest, stepped forward. "Intruders," he called, "by what right are you here?"

"By the right of combat," Helaine answered. She gestured at the two fallen guards. "We have defeated your watchers and claim the right to an audience."

The guard eyed her with caution. "You know our ways," he said softly.

"She ought to," muttered Score. "You're a product of her imagination."

"Yes," Helaine said. "We come here only to seek directions. A friend of ours is missing and must be found. We wish to know the closest way to finding him."

A female guard stepped forward, a slight sneer on her face. "The one called Pixel?" she asked. "Yes, we know where he can be found. And if you wait a short while, it will be within our halls."

Score didn't quite get this, but evidently Helaine did. "He is that close to death, then?" she demanded.

"Yes," the woman agreed. "I doubt you could save him in time. Conserve your strength, because you will be joining him soon."

"I had thought the Fair Folk had honor," Helaine said scornfully. "Do you now threaten us?"

"Not us," the man replied. "But you cannot leave this world. And, sooner or later, you must rest."

"What are you talking about?" Score demanded. He was getting very sick of these Fair Folk and their veiled threats. "We can leave any time. All we have to do is to summon up a Portal."

"Your Portals will not work on Zarathan," the guard answered. "One with greater power than you has blocked their access."

Score was suddenly very worried. "Can this jerk be telling the truth?" he asked Helaine.

"The Fair Folk *always* tell the truth," Helaine said simply. "They scorn to lie." She looked worried, too. "But if we can't make a Portal, then we *are* doomed, just as they claim."

"I'll worry about that when the time comes," Score decided. "I've got enough to worry about right now. The first thing we have to do is to find Pixel." He glared at the female guard. "Look, we're asking you to help us."

"We have no reason to help humans," she said scornfully. "Fight your own battles, seek your own power, and leave us out of your affairs."

"It's too late for that," Score informed her. "You're stuck in this role right now. So be a sport and help us out."

"And if we do not wish to?" the male guard asked. "How will you compel us?"

Score had taken about as much as he was going to from these snobs. He turned to Helaine. "Look, Your Mightiness, being polite to these guys doesn't seem to be working. I say we kick some of their pretty butts."

Helaine suddenly smiled. "Score, you're a genius!"

"I know I am," he agreed, confused. "About what in particular?"

"About these Fair Folk being pretty," Helaine answered. "That's what the Cormac's puzzle meant." She gestured at the shield. "These Fair Folk are beautiful to look at, but corrupt inside. We have to make them see themselves. If they look at their reflections, they will find defect."

"Got you!" Score agreed, catching on. He pulled the shield off his arm, and turned it so that the polished inside was facing the Fair Folk. It was acting like a mirror. . . .

The female guard tried to look away, but it was too late. With a scream, she saw her own reflection in the shield. Score didn't know what it was that she saw, but it had to be the cold heartlessness inside her.

She began to change. Her golden hair turned pale and strawlike. Her perfect features began to crinkle and wrinkle. Her skin puckered and shrank, bones sticking out of her skin. Her golden eyes went black, and she hunched forward. She mewed piteously, now looking as if she were hundreds of years old.

Appalled, Score turned the shield back around. She looked awful, on the verge of death. He hadn't expected this to happen! Neither, apparently, had the other Fair Folk. They backed away from the old crone, shaking and pale.

"We can do that to you all, and to your city," Helaine said coldly. "Unless you show us the way that we must take."

The male guard nodded desperately. "We agree," he said quickly. "Come with us, and keep that mirror chained!"

As she passed him, Helaine murmured into Score's ear, "Don't be so upset. She's not real, don't forget."

He *had* forgotten for a moment, because the woman had seemed to be so alive. But she was just an animated dream, nothing more. A potentially dangerous one, of course. Shaken despite this knowledge, Score hurried past the woman, trying to ignore her wailing and her outstretched hand. This magic business was very hard to take sometimes.

The other guards hurried them through the streets of the city. Silent citizens watched them pass, apparently aware of the power that the two intruders possessed. Fear and hatred were in their eyes, but none of them made a move toward the humans.

"Can we trust them not to attack?" he whispered to Helaine.

"Yes," she answered. "They promised to show us to the right exit. And the Fair Folk always keep their word."

Score nodded. But something troubled him about what she had said, even though the guards had promised to show them to the right exit.

The city was probably a place of much noise and fun, normally. But it was silent and brooding as they passed through the streets, which were literally paved with gold. As they walked, Score noticed that there was no glass or polished metal of any kind that might act as a mirror. The gold glittered, but it didn't hold reflections. These Fair Folk really couldn't stand themselves, it seemed.

Soon they were out of the city and heading toward the cavern wall again. Ahead was an opening like a cave. The male guard gestured toward it. "That will take you to the surface, close to where you will find your friend," he told them. "Go now, and don't look back."

Helaine nodded, and led the way toward the opening. Score followed, his mind bothered by something.

And then it clicked: The Fair Folk always kept their word, and they had led them to the right path.

They hadn't promised anything else.

Helaine's sense of danger kicked in at the same second that Score realized this. He whirled around, knowing why the Fair Folk hadn't wanted them to look back. The guards had their spears ready to throw, aiming to kill them both from behind. With a roar of anger, Score held the reversed shield at them.

They all screamed, dropping their weapons and trying to cover their eyes. It was no use: They couldn't escape their own reflections.

"People who are liars at heart always tell the truth," he grunted. "Just enough of it to make the lie worse." He slammed the shield down into the soil, wedging it to protect his and Helaine's backs. The Fair Folk were screaming and aging. "Come on," he said to Helaine. "That will stop them from following us."

Helaine gave him an admiring look. "Clever," she said approvingly. "That's the perfect solution to watching our backs." Still, she had her sword drawn and she made no move to put it away. Hurrying, she set off through the tunnel.

Score took one look back over his shoulder. The Fair Folk weren't so fair now: They were hunched, moaning and howling, aged and bent. It served them right for being so deceitful. Still, Score couldn't help shuddering at their fates. Even if they were no more than animated dreams.

He plunged into the tunnel after Helaine. They might be closer to Pixel now, but there were still plenty of dangers to be faced. . . .

CHAPTER 11

Helaine led the way upward again. She knew how long they had already been on Zarathan, and how tired they were both getting. The only thing that still kept them going was the need to find Pixel. But what if he had already given in and rested? He had to be as exhausted as they were — possibly more so, as he hadn't had the chance to eat that they had. Since he didn't know about the dangers here, it was all too possible that he might have tried to get some rest already. . . . He could be dead by now.

No! She wouldn't believe that. She couldn't! She had to believe that he was still alive, and still in need of help. Grimly, she pressed on as fast as she dared. It wouldn't do Pixel any good if she tired herself out before they found him. Whatever else happened, they still had Destiny to face.

More so than she had thought, obviously. The Fair Folk had said that she was blocking the formation of a Portal off Zarathan. If they were correct — and she had no reason to doubt them — then it meant that simply finding Pixel and then returning home wasn't an option. They had to take Destiny out, too.

This really bothered Helaine. Even though she knew that Destiny had been plotting against them from the start, Helaine still couldn't bring herself to hate the girl. She had been treated very badly by the Triad, and sent to Earth without her powers. In one sense, Destiny's anger was partly Helaine's fault. Even though she, Pixel, and Score weren't actually the Triad, they had been formed from the Triad, and in some respects had the same personalities as the tyrants. Helaine shuddered as she remembered seeing Eremin, and knowing that she could have become such a monster.

She still could, of course. The potential was inside her to become as cold, arrogant, and heartless as Eremin had been. Only now that she was warned, she was determined that it would never happen. Hard as it sometimes was, she tried to be gentler, more loving, and less standoffish. The thought of ending up like Eremin terrified her.

So she could empathize at least in part with Destiny's hatred of the Triad and her desire for freedom. It was Destiny's other obsession that Helaine couldn't fathom. Why had she tried to kill Score? And why had she kidnapped Pixel and brought him here? She obviously had a reason, tied to her desire for power. Helaine couldn't see what it might be.

Working things out was Pixel's game, really. Helaine knew that if they could free him, he'd undoubtedly be able to figure everything out. She realized that she missed having him around. She'd gotten used to his calm, sensible manner, and even to his tendency to be totally unrealistic at times. He made her smile, and she appreciated that.

Score, on the other hand, often infuriated her with his sometimes nasty wit and his habit of arguing with everything she said. Still, he had grown on her. So much so that when she had sought guidance in finding Pixel, the first thing that she had seen had nothing to do with Pixel, and everything to do with Score. She clamped her mind shut on that. There was absolutely no way she was going to tell Score what she had seen. . . .

Helaine glanced at him and saw that he was lost in his own thoughts. "Worrying about Pixel?" she asked him gently.

"Yeah." Score gave her an odd look. "Listen, if you ever tell him this, I'll deny every last word of it. But I'm really worried for him. I'm not used to having friends, and now I have two. I couldn't ask for any better buddies. The thought of losing one, especially to this lousy mind-sucking planet, really hurts." He shook his head. "That's the problem with making friends, you know. You give those people the power to hurt you."

"Yes," she agreed, touched by his feelings. "But you also give them the greater power to make you happy. I think that outweighs the possible hurt."

"I'd like to think so," Score agreed, brightening a little. "You know, you're okay for a . . ."

"Girl?" Helaine suggested, her lips curling slightly. He'd had a real problem with that at first, but he'd seemed to be getting over it.

Score grinned. "Actually, I was going to say *pompous donkey*, but *girl* will do just fine."

Helaine pretended to growl at him, but she knew he didn't really mean it. It was just his way of keeping his spirits up. She felt good. Maybe there was hope for Score yet.

The tunnel ended and they emerged into another burial chamber. This time, it was still occupied. There was the body of a chieftain laid out on the shelf, his sword clasped across his chest, his spear and shield beside him.

"Are we going to have to fight this guy to get out?" Score whispered.

"No," she answered, equally quietly. "We don't need permission to leave, only to enter."

"Well, that's the first bit of cheerful news I've heard today," Score said, encouraged. He followed her out of the chamber and up to the surface once again.

It was still nighttime and foggy. The ground continued to shudder beneath their feet at regular intervals, and it looked to Helaine as if they'd simply come out where they had gone in. But she was confident that the Fair Folk hadn't lied, and that she and Score were close to Pixel.

There was the howl of a hunting hound in the air. Helaine glanced around, trying to work out the direction it was coming from.

"Great," Score muttered. "Another of your rotten nightmares. What's this one going to be about?"

Helaine shook her head. "I don't have problems with dogs," she said. "Actually, I'm very fond of them. My father always kept wolfhounds, and I loved to play with them."

Score frowned. "If they're not *your* nightmare, then . . ." His voice trailed off. Helaine realized the answer the same second he did. "Pixel!" they chorused, recalling his story of being attacked on Calomir by the ravenous hounds.

"Come on," Helaine said, drawing her sword. "I'm sure the noise came from this direction." She set off at a run, listening carefully. She heard the dogs baying. The noise was getting louder. They were definitely heading in the right direction. Panting, tired to the bone, she forced her body to keep moving. If the hounds were crying like that, it must mean that Pixel was still alive! This certainty gave her extra strength from somewhere, and she pressed on, trying to see through darkness and fog.

Finally, her legs aching and her lungs on fire, she could make out shapes ahead. There was a flash of light and the yelp of a startled dog. It had to be Pixel, fighting off the pack! She saw several low, slinking forms and let out as loud a whoop as she could. Just behind her, Score howled out a challenge, too.

The dogs whirled to face their new foes, and Helaine could suddenly see Pixel. He'd been bitten in the leg, and his blood was dripping down to the ground, inciting the dogs to even more frenzied attacks. She yelled again and plunged into the battle, swinging her sword at anything that moved. One killer dog fell away, yelping, its side gashed open. Another jumped at her, its teeth going for her throat. She thrust out her sword, spearing it through the right shoulder. With a jerk, she tossed the dog aside, where it lay whimpering.

Score was using magic on whatever was in range. Using his emerald, he was opening pits in the ground too deep for the dogs to scramble out again. Pixel was still using his firepower to send the dogs scurrying for cover. Helaine preferred the simpler method of hacking at them until they were too injured to fight further.

Finally, the dogs were all defeated. They were either sliced and whimpering, or else stuck down in pits, slavering furiously and barking their brains out, unable to get free. Helaine sighed and wiped the blood off her sword and slid it back into her scabbard. She felt so drained, she could hardly stand. Then Pixel grabbed her and hugged her.

"I knew you'd be looking for me!" he exclaimed. "I am *so* glad to see you both!" His eyes were red, and he looked on the verge of collapse, too.

"You hug me like that," Score warned him, "and I'll knock some of your teeth out. A simple 'Hi, good to see you' is fine." But he was grinning as he said it.

Pixel blushed and let Helaine go. "Uh, sorry about that. I guess I got a bit carried away."

"I don't blame you," Helaine said kindly. She gave him a quick peck on the cheek. "We're so glad to have you back with us before you went to sleep."

"Sleep?" Pixel stifled a yawn. "I've been thinking about that for the longest time. But it's hard to snooze while you're being attacked by a pack of hungry dogs. Mind you, now that we're together again, we could take turns and —"

"NO!" Helaine and Score yelled at the same instant. Then she let Score explain the problem.

Pixel went pale. "Wow. It's just dumb luck I didn't get any rest," he said. "Destiny didn't breathe a word about that to me. She must have wanted me to succumb."

"She's trying to kill you," Helaine said. "Just like she tried to kill Score. She's homicidal."

"No," Pixel said thoughtfully. "If she'd wanted to kill me, she could have done it anytime. Don't forget, she had a knife at my throat when we arrived here. One tug, and I'd have been dead. And then she chained me up in the labyrinth. . . ." He explained his adventures, and finished thoughtfully, "I thought I'd tricked her and escaped without her knowing it. But now I'm not so sure. I don't think she was trying to kill me, as such. And I don't think that was what she was aiming to do with Score on Earth, either."

"Huh?" Score snorted. "Pixel, I think one of those dogs must have had rabies and you're delirious. What else was she trying to do? She was weakening me until I died."

"No," Pixel said with conviction. "If she'd wanted to kill you, she could have destroyed the locket. *That* would have killed you. Instead, she simply weakened you, and then left the locket where I was almost sure to find it. I think she wanted you weakened, not dead. And me, too. Whatever the force is on Zarathan that saps your mind and soul when you sleep, I think she *intended* to use it to weaken me."

"But why?" asked Score, confused. "This isn't making very much sense yet."

"We need help," Helaine decided reluctantly. "Maybe Shanara has had time to find something out. I'm going to contact her and see." She pulled out her crystal.

Score stopped her, a worried look on his face. "We're all exhausted from this place," he objected. "This is going to tire you even more."

Touched by his concern, Helaine shook his hand free. "We really need information," she pointed out. "Otherwise we're doomed. I have to take the chance, or we'll all die."

Pixel sighed. "Score, she's right. There's just too much that we don't know. I don't like the risk, but what else can we do?"

"Nothing," Score admitted, his shoulders sagging. "I just don't like it."

"Nor do I," admitted Helaine honestly. Then she focused her thoughts through the agate, even though she could feel her strength draining as she did so. *Shanara? Are you there?*

Helaine! came the wizard's immediate response. *Thank goodness you contacted us! Oracle has important news for you, but we couldn't find you! Stay there, he's going to follow your signal to you!*

Helaine managed to keep the communication open for a few more seconds, and then had to stop, on the verge of collapse.

"Ah!" said Oracle's voice as he strode out of the darkness to join them. "It sounds like I've timed my entrance perfectly for once."

"Oracle," Helaine said, smiling, "am I glad to see you. Can you explain anything that's going on here?"

"Some," he admitted. "I've been doing some research into Destiny's background. Well, you know that she worked for the Triad, and was then sent to Earth by them. She claims it was as an experiment to see if the transfer of souls to babies was possible.

Well, in one sense, that was true. But there's more to it than that. In fact, *she* was the one who betrayed the Triad to Sarman. She was giving him information to help him defeat them. In return, he had promised to marry her and share the rule over the Diadem with her. In fact, he had absolutely no intention of honoring the agreement.

"What he in fact did was to betray her to the Triad, exposing her treachery without them knowing where the information came from. He didn't want her around when he came to take over, and he decided that having them deal with her was the best move. As a result, that's why they exiled her to Earth and tried to make certain she'd stay there."

Score nodded. "I *knew* she wasn't telling us the whole truth. So she wasn't just some innocent pawn in the Triad's plans, then. She deserved her fate."

"And it makes some sense of what she's doing here," Pixel said. "She was after ruling the Diadem from the beginning, and now she's after extra power to try again. Now that Sarman and the Triad are finished, she's trying to seize her chance."

"It sounds reasonable," agreed Helaine. "But why is she here on Zarathan? What's so special about this world?"

"I may have a clue," Oracle replied. "Though, frankly, I don't know if it's relevant or not. Since I'm immaterial, I went into the gem room on Jewel." This was the room where Sarman had set up his huge representation of the worlds of the Diadem. Each world was represented by a gemstone, and a single life-force from each planet involved was infused into the jewel. Through this, the flow of magic holding the Diadem together was maintained. The three of them had sealed it off against intruders, but Oracle was rather special. "I examined the gemstone representing Zarathan. It's a garnet, and there's something very odd about it. All of the others contain a single life-force; this one doesn't. All that's in it is a very small piece of a life-force. It's enough to power the jewel, but it's as if it's just a small portion of a much larger life-form."

Pixel's eyes widened, and Helaine could see that he was putting together the facts. He was brilliant at doing this, deducing everything from small hints. "Of course!" he breathed. "Now I see what's happening!" He turned to Helaine and Score. "There's nothing living on this planet at all, is there? No animals, not even a blade of grass."

"Right," Helaine agreed. "Everything else we've met so far is nothing more than a dream made solid." She frowned. "I see your point: What life-force could Sarman have taken? Unless there used to be life here, and it got wiped out somehow?"

"It's still here," Pixel said excitedly. "Only not where we're looking for it." The ground shook again in one of the regular tremors. "It's not *on* the planet, it *is* the planet."

Helaine was stunned. "But . . . but that's not possible," she protested weakly.

"Yes, it is," Pixel insisted. "The earthquakes aren't really tremors — that's the creature breathing. It's a living creature, the size of a planet."

"You've got rocks in your head," Score protested. "Look, we're standing on soil, and there are rocks and an atmosphere and everything. This is a planet, not a turtle or something."

"Because of its size," Pixel explained. "It's the size of a planet, so it can gather matter from space. On all worlds, there's constantly meteorites falling, contributing mass to them. Soil and rocks can come from those. The atmosphere is produced by the creature itself. Since it's so big, the air wouldn't escape."

"A creature the size of a planet," Helaine said in wonder. "That's almost unbelievable. Except so much has happened to us recently that I'm reluctant to say it's impossible."

"Well, I'm still not convinced," Score said stubbornly. "If it's alive, what's it doing?"

"Sleeping," Pixel answered with a laugh. "Dreaming. *That's* what the trap here is. Just as the creature is so much larger than normal creatures, so are its dreams. They're so much more powerful than our own. It taps into our minds, and makes our dreams seem to come true in its own dreams. And if we fall asleep, its much more powerful mind absorbs our own."

Helaine shivered. "Scary," she admitted. "So, if you're right, we simply have to leave. Only the Fair Folk claim that Destiny is blocking our forming a Portal, so we can't escape."

"So, what's she doing here if you're right?" Score demanded of Pixel. "What's she up to?"

"She must be trying to tap into the power of Zarathan somehow," Pixel replied. "She's still after control of the Diadem, and thinks she can get it from here."

"If this planet-creature is as powerful as you think," Oracle put in, "then perhaps she can. You three are essentially the Triad, you know. If she can get Zarathan to absorb your minds, and then somehow control it, she might be able to rule the Diadem."

"You three are the Triad?"

Helaine spun around, her eyes widening as Destiny seemed to appear out of thin air. Her face was twisted in fury. She must have been listening to them invisibly, and heard what Oracle had just said.

"If that's true," Destiny said with a cold, savage smile, "then watching Zarathan absorb you is going to be even more delightful than I had imagined."

CHAPTER 12

Pixel stared at Destiny in shock. "You were following me all the time!" he exclaimed.

"Of course I was, you fool," she snapped. "I wanted to be on hand when you collapsed and slept." She raised an eyebrow. "You've got to be *really* tired by now."

He was, but he wasn't going to admit this to her. "I can stand it," he insisted. "You can't possibly defeat the three of us together."

"I don't have to *defeat* you," Destiny answered. "All I have to do is outlast you. And I shall. All three of you will fall asleep before I do, and then I'll have my revenge." She smiled again. "I didn't realize that I'd get a chance to pay you back for what you did to me. I'm *so* glad I can."

"It wasn't *us*," Score said. "We're not the Triad. We're as much their victims as you are. That business they did with sending you to be reborn on Earth in a new body was what they did to us, too. We're a portion of them, I guess. A potential. What might one day turn into them. But we won't, because we despise everything they stood for."

"In one sense," Pixel added, "we're the revenge you wanted on the Triad. We're preventing them from ever existing again, simply by being ourselves."

Destiny shrugged. "I don't really believe that. And even if I did, it makes no difference to me. I need your power for myself. You see, I've been to Zarathan before. I saw what it did to other people. It absorbed my sister's mind, the way it wants to absorb yours. Only, just as it did so, I saw an interesting chance. As Zarathan puts you to sleep, but before it can absorb you, the human mind goes pliant. I discovered I could reach in and take the power of that person at the moment of absorption. Zarathan will get your minds and souls, while I will get your magical power."

Pixel stared at her in disgust. "You allowed the planet to kill your own sister, just so you could steal her power? You're sicker than I thought!"

"I *needed* the power, just as I need yours," Destiny answered. "And I will get it. Now that I am back on Zarathan, I have my powers back again. The Triad's spells no longer bind me. I'm a match for the three of you, if you choose to fight me. But you won't be able to. I have no intention of waiting around so that you can try and beat me. I've made certain that you can't get off this planet by forming a Portal. All I have to do is to outwait you. You'll fall asleep, and then I'll have you. I've set up a little sleep spell to help you along. Enjoy!" With a final laugh, she vanished again.

Pixel whipped out his ruby, and focused on finding her again. She was halfway around the planet now. He sighed, and replaced his gem. "She's gotten away from us for the moment," he reported. He felt exhausted. "And she's right — we can't prevent ourselves from sleeping for very much longer. Every time we use our magic, it tires us even more. We're going to collapse soon."

Helaine nodded, and winced with the effort. "Yes," she agreed sadly. "I'm badly in need of a rest. I don't know how much longer I can go on."

"Coffee!" Score said, urgently. "We've got to stay awake. We have to outlast her! All we have to do is stay awake longer than she can."

"But she's been more careful than we have," Pixel answered, stifling a yawn. "She knew what she

152

was doing, and how to plan it. She's deliberately tired us out, while she's still fresh. We'll never make it. We can't possibly outlast her, Score."

"We can't just give up!" Score cried. "We can't let her beat us. Pixel, *you're* far smarter than she is! Helaine, you're too brave to give up now! And I'm too stubborn. There *must* be something we can do to defeat her!" He ruined the effect of his pep talk by yawning widely. "I'd better make us some coffee. That'll help."

"No!" Pixel said urgently. "The more magic you do, the more tired you'll get. It'll counter the effects of the coffee in keeping you awake."

"Maybe," Score agreed stubbornly. "But it'll help the two of you. Maybe you'll be able to beat her, even if I can't."

Helaine laid a hand on his shoulder. "It's very brave of you to offer to sacrifice yourself to save us," she said. "But we're all in this together. No coffee."

"Idiot," Score muttered, but not too loudly.

Pixel found it incredibly hard staying awake. He really needed to rest, and even knowing that it would kill him if he did wasn't enough to fight off the sleepiness. He could see that the other two were having just as hard a time of it. Staying awake wasn't the easiest thing in the world.

He tried to focus his mind. There had to be *something* they could do. Some way around this trap. Some way to beat Destiny. But he was simply too tired to think straight. Maybe, after a short nap . . .

No! His head jerked up, and he realized how close he had come to falling asleep. It was essential to stay awake. . . .

Helaine stumbled and Score grabbed her, shaking her hard. "Stay on your feet!" he insisted. "If you sit down, it'll be too easy to drop off!"

"I'm so tired," she complained feebly.

"We *all* are!" Score yelled at her. "Don't tell me you're being a quitter! You chickenhearted little jerk!"

That brought fire into her eyes. Her fingers went for her sword, before she realized why Score had been so rude. "Thanks," she said. "I needed that."

"And I've been dying to say it," Score said, yawning.

It was no good. Pixel could feel the grip of sleep tightening around them all. He needed some way to wake them all up. . . .

And then he had the answer.

Grinning like a maniac, he howled, "We don't have to stay awake!"

"Huh?" Score gave him a bleary glare. "You *want* us to fall asleep?"

"No." Excitement helped Pixel to focus his thoughts. "We're going about this the wrong way. We shouldn't be focusing on keeping ourselves awake.

We should be acting on removing the problem." He saw blank stares from both of them and Oracle. "The planet's the key," Pixel said. "We're being drawn into its dreams. So what we have to do is to wake it up!"

All three stared at him for a moment, their faces completely blank. Then Oracle grinned and Score shrugged.

"Can we do that?" asked Helaine practically.

"I'm sure we can," Pixel answered. "We can link up and use your agate to contact the mind of this creature. If Zarathan wakes up, then we'll be out of danger."

"Maybe," Score mumbled. "Unless it gets out of bed on the wrong side and is all cranky before it has its first cup of coffee."

"We have to take that chance," Pixel insisted. "Because otherwise we're doomed."

"I agree," Helaine said, taking out her agate. "It's the only chance we've got. Literally, because using the agate is likely to drain most of our remaining energy."

Oracle nodded. "You won't have enough strength left to form a Portal," he said. "I'll go back to Shanara, and have her make one the second she can. Even if you wake Zarathan up, you'll still have to face Destiny, you know."

"One crisis at a time," Pixel said. Oracle nodded and vanished. Pixel turned to his friends. "Link hands," he ordered. "Concentrate."

This was mostly Helaine's chore. She was their communications expert. He and Score were just there to add to her feeble strength with what little they had left themselves. Together, they clasped hands and then focused on the agate.

Pixel could feel their combined strengths linking up, and then Helaine sent out the call to the mind of the planet-creature: "WAKE UP!!!"

Pixel concentrated with all of his remaining strength, keeping nothing back in reserve. If this failed, the three of them were doomed. None of them had the strength left for any further attempts. Weariness washed over him, but he forced his mind into focus.

Together, they probed down into the mind of the planet-creature. Pixel could feel some sort of very alien mind beneath them. Strange thoughts flickered across the sleeping brain, nightmares and dreams that flittered and changed every second. Pixel was aware that the planet's mind was vast, with huge depths of thought that were completely foreign to mankind. But there were similiarities, enough so that Pixel could push their probe forward.

There! This was the equivalent of the human sleep center, the portion of the brain controlling dormancy. With all of his failing strength, Pixel pushed Helaine's intense screaming into this area, and felt a definite response from the strange mind.

There was the shock of something reacting that almost broke them free. Pixel had a momentary glimpse into that huge, alien mind as the call lodged itself in Zarathan's consciousness, and felt the creature react.

And then the link was broken and he was thrown off his feet as the ground shook. This wasn't one of the minor tremors the planet had been going through on a regular basis, but a major quake. The ground heaved and churned, tossing them all apart. Cracks started to appear in the earth, and the quake became more and more powerful.

Destiny suddenly appeared in front of him. She was looking around wildly, struggling to stay on her own feet. "What have you done, you idiots?" she screamed.

"The only thing we could do," Pixel answered. "We've woken the planet up."

"No!" Destiny howled. "You maniacs! Don't you understand what you're doing? Zarathan isn't an *animal* — it's an *egg*!"

An egg.... Pixel suddenly realized what she meant. "And it's breaking out of its shell now that it's woken up," he gasped. "Oh, no!"

"Oh, *yes!*" Destiny snarled.

The earth was splitting, shattering, and heaving all around them. Pixel was thrown against a rock, and he felt a sharp pain in his back. The planet was going to break apart as Zarathan hatched....

"Drop the spell that's keeping us here!" he called to Destiny. "Then we can all escape. Do it!"

"Never!" Destiny howled. "I'm not going to let you go again. I'll have my revenge — and my power!"

"You'll be *dead* if we stay here!" Score called out. "What's the point in that? Take down the barrier, and we can talk this over on Treen!"

"No!" Destiny screamed over the sound of shattering earth. "You can all die here, then! You're not escaping me again."

"She's gone crazy!" Helaine snarled, clutching a large rock in an attempt to avoid being tossed aside. "There's no point in talking to her."

"Die!" Destiny yelled, obviously deranged. She simply couldn't face another of her plans being ruined. She was beyond help now. But she still had them trapped here.

The ground was shaking harder and harder, and great cracks were appearing all over the landscape.

Pixel narrowly avoided falling into one of the fissures. He hadn't been able to see the bottom of it. Rocks danced on the shaking ground, and he was being flung wildly about.

Any moment now, the crust of the planet would shatter and the creature that was Zarathan would emerge. That emergence would kill them all.

A bolt of fire narrowly missed Pixel. He gasped, and saw that Destiny was preparing to throw a second blast. "What are you doing?" he screamed.

"If I can't absorb you, then I'll kill you!" Destiny howled back over the sound of the planet fragmenting.

"She's totally crazy!" Score gasped. "This is no time to fight!"

Pixel realized that Score was right; faced with the ruin of another of her plans, Destiny had become completely unhinged. Ignoring the destruction all around her, her only thought was to kill her enemies. And none of them had any strength left at all to perform any kind of magic right now. They were helpless before Destiny, who had conserved her own strength.

As she drew back her arm to throw the next fireball, Destiny's face was lit with the glow of madness. Then the ground lurched beneath her feet, throwing her aim completely off. The fireball exploded thirty feet above her three intended targets.

Something was emerging from the ground, fighting to be free. Pixel caught a glimpse of what looked like a tentacle of some kind, uncurling and pushing at the solid rocks. The ground was in constant motion now, and Pixel was being tossed about like he was on a small raft in a tidal wave. It took all of his strength simply to cling on, to avoid being thrown to his death. Close by, Helaine and Score were similarly locked into position. Both looked as drained and scared as he knew he did. They simply couldn't take very much more of this.

"No!" Destiny yelled, furious. She snarled something that the wind snatched away. The air was in as great a motion now as the earth, whipping and tearing at them all as they clung onto their fragile holds. A hurricane was in the making as the creature that was Zarathan struggled to break free.

Pixel wondered if he had *really* had a good idea — or whether he had simply hastened their deaths.

Rocks churned and groaned about them, rising and falling, grinding and shattering. His hands were taking a terrible battering, and his muscles were all screaming out in pain. He couldn't hold on for very much longer. The only reason he'd lasted this long was that with the waking of Zarathan the relentless pressure to sleep and dream had diminished. But his strength was still almost spent. In this whirling maelstrom of air and earth, none of them could hold out for very much longer.

The planet was shattering around them. More of the mountainous tentacles clawed at the surface of the planet, uncurling and striving to be free. The vast mind was now fully awake and intent on hatching. And he, Helaine, Score, and Destiny were far too insignificant for it to notice. They were less than fleas on its skin.

Death was barely moments away, Pixel realized. His fingers were starting to lose their grip, and he knew he would be thrown from his precarious perch any second now, and then plunge into the crushing rocks.

The ground shattered again, great crevices running across the surface. Destiny screamed as the ground vanished beneath her feet. She toppled backward into the fissure, howling wildly. Even though she was crazy and out for his blood, Pixel was shocked to see her fall from his sight.

And a second later, the gash of a Portal appeared in the air in front of him.

Destiny must have died in the fall, freeing her spell, and Shanara had come through just in time! Pixel struggled toward the gash in space, looking around for his friends.

Helaine was close behind him, crawling wearily across the shaking ground. Score staggered along on his feet, though barely, forcing himself to move on. Pixel reached out and grabbed Helaine. With a push, he propelled her through the Portal. Then he managed to stagger to his feet and grab Score. "Come on," he growled, and he threw the two of them into the gap.

The last thing he saw as the Portal closed behind them was the ground shattering completely, and *something* moving in the depths as Zarathan broke out of its shell. . . .

EPILOGUE

Shanara looked in on her patients, a slight smile on her face. Blink was perched on her shoulder as they checked each room in Aranak's tower in turn. Helaine, Score, and Pixel were all sleeping peacefully, their bodies masses of sores and cuts, but with serene expressions on their faces as they finally all got the rest they needed.

"They remind me of you," Shanara told Blink. "Only they have a reason to be so tired. You're just plain lazy."

"Me?" Blink sounded shocked. "It's because I work so hard while I'm awake that I get so tired. Who is it that's been keeping track of Zarathan anyway?"

Shanara sniffed, and tried to tickle Blink with a strand of her bright green hair. "Grouchy. Just because I actually have you doing something at last. How is our little planet-sized creature doing?"

"Quite well," Blink answered. "It was almost ready to hatch on its own accord anyway, which was obviously why Destiny was in such a hurry. So it's doing rather well. I just wonder what a creature that size will find to eat out there in space, though."

"Typical," Shanara complained. "You can always find a way to return any conversation to the subject of food."

"Speaking of which . . ." Blink began.

"Don't say it," she warned him. "You just ate. Now, all you have to do is stay awake and help me to begin healing our friends' wounds. By the time they wake up again, I want them all to be as good as new."

"What's the hurry?" Blink complained. "Haven't they earned a rest?"

"More than earned it," Shanara agreed. "However . . . who knows what will happen next?"

ABOUT THE AUTHOR

JOHN PEEL is the author of numerous best-selling novels for young adults, including installments in the Star Trek, Are You Afraid of the Dark?, and Where in the World Is Carmen Sandiego? series. He is also the author of many acclaimed novels of science fiction, horror, and suspense.

Mr. Peel currently lives on the outer rim of the Diadem, on the planet popularly known as Earth.